A bit of Christmas

6 Christian Short Stories
Celebrating the Season

by Angela K. Couch, Kathleen Neely, Emily Conrad,
Kari Fischer, and Allison K. Garcia

Edited by Lynellen D.S. Perry

HopeSprings Books
http://www.HopeSpringsBooks.com

Cover design by HopeSprings Books
Cover art photo ©iStockphoto.com/picalotta
Scripture quoted by permission. Unless otherwise designated, all quotations are from THE HOLY BIBLE: NEW INTERNATIONAL VERSION®. NIV®. Copyright © 1973, 1978, 1984 by Biblica. All rights reserved worldwide.

Published in the United States of America. By HopeSprings Books, an imprint of Chalfont House Publishing.
www.HopeSpirngsBooks.com
www.ChalfontHouse.com

Publisher's Note: The short stories in this anthology are a work of fiction. Names, characters, places, and incidents are either products of the author's imagination or used fictitiously. Al characters are fictional, and any similarity to people living or dead is purely coincidental.

Paperback ISBN 978-1-938708-77-0
Ebook ISBN 978-1-938708-78-7
Printed in the United States of America.

Table of Contents

Introduction

Introduction

When we first started talking about forming the Virginia Chapter of American Christian Fiction Writers (ACFW), I knew I wanted to see us offer a short story contest. Happily, the rest of the Chapter's Board was excited about that, too, and so the first annual ACFW Virginia Short Story Contest was born. Since 2015 was also the first year of our Chapter, we knew the publication would have to happen toward the end of the year, making Christmas a natural theme for all the stories to share.

Out of those initial musings came the book you now hold in your hands, a collection of the Chapter's favorite Christmas-themed short stories. It's our earnest hope that reading them provides a little warmth and cheer in the spirit of celebrating our Savior's birth.

We're grateful to Lynellen Perry, President of Chalfont House and their fiction imprint, HopeSprings Books, for her willingness to publish these winning stories. We're also grateful to the national ACFW for allowing us to host this contest with publication as one of the prizes.

Most of all, we're grateful to you, the reader, for taking the time to purchase and read these stories. For several of these authors, this collection is their first publication and I know they'd be thrilled to hear your thoughts on the stories via a review on Amazon, Goodreads, or any other retail site, or through personal contact on their Facebook, Twitter or other social media.

If you are an aspiring author (or an already published one!) who enjoys crafting short stories, we invite you to keep an eye on our website, www.acfwvirginia.com, for announcements about our 2016 Short Story Contest.

Blessings as you celebrate Christ's birth,
Elizabeth Maddrey, ACFW Virginia President

I Heard
the Bells

by Angela K. Couch
(First Place)

Virginia, December 1864

Gabriel's heart pounded. Two days ago, he'd marched against hundreds of Confederate guns, yet facing death hadn't affected him like the sight of that cozy farm house, smoke rising from the chimney, a light glowing in one of the windows. He paused at the edge of the orchard, the trees' bare arms extending over his head. His breath billowed in the air. Dusk had introduced a biting chill and turned a gentle shower into flecks of white... just in time for Christmas.

Dropping his gaze from the frame house to the faded and muddied blue uniform he wore, Gabriel dragged his hat from his head. What was he doing here? The farm appeared to be faring well enough. His family was probably fine. Best for him to walk away.

Since when did he do what was best? Or easiest, for that matter.

With his hat tucked under his arm, he buried his hands in his pockets and jogged the short distance remaining. He wrapped his fingers around the latch, then froze. This was no longer his home. According to Pa, he wasn't even a member of the family anymore.

He knocked.

His pulse thundered as footsteps padded toward the door. It opened with a creak. The tall, wiry frame of one of the most handsome women he'd known stood motionless with a backdrop of light from the fireplace as the sun continued its quick escape. She stared, eyes wide and brimming.

"Mama."

She blinked rapidly, sweeping loose strands of hair from her cheeks. The deep honey tones that had graced her head appeared faded, now laced with white. "Lord, be praised. Gabriel? Can that really be you?"

He nodded. His teeth gritted against the burning behind his eyes.

She opened her arms and he stepped into them, returning the embrace. "What are you doing here? And in that uniform? It can't be safe."

"Probably isn't, but our troops are camped only miles away, and with no enemy lines between here and there..." He glanced around the room. The long table, the large stone fireplace, Mama's rocker across from Pa's high-backed chair—everything exactly as it had been three years ago, except empty. "Where's Pa?"

"He's dead, son."

Gabriel's head snapped back to his mother. "Dead? How?"

"Battle. In Pennsylvania, just over six months ago. Near a town called Gettysburg, they said." She squeezed his hand. "He left shortly after you."

"Gettysburg?" The word slammed into his chest, ripping apart his lungs. He fought for a breath. "Not Gettysburg."

She nodded. "Lawrence was there, as well."

No. He couldn't be old enough to be a part of this. "Did he...?" Gabriel couldn't finish.

"He's fine. He's even come home since. His platoon has been through the area recently."

Gabriel's gut twisted. What if...? The fact that they had all fought at Gettysburg was bad enough. "I'm so sorry, Mama."

He pulled her back into an embrace and buried his face in her neck.

"Oh, my boy, you have nothing to apologize for." She braced his shoulders. "I don't have a side. I never have. I made up my mind about that the minute you walked out the door and pointed your horse north."

North.

Everything had seemed so clear in his mind when he'd left, but the line between who was right and who was wrong had since been drowned in blood and heaped upon with corpses. Though in all likelihood the Union would soon have their victory, Gabriel was too weary to muster much more than thanks to God that it would finally be over.

He straightened, seeking his mother's face. She smiled at him, dark eyes shining.

"I'm proud of you, son. You followed your heart, and did what you felt was right. And look at you..." She ran her finger over the gold bar on his shoulder strap.

Her praise only increased the ache in his chest, but he answered the question she'd hung between them. "First lieutenant."

"Lieutenant Morgan. What mother wouldn't be proud?" She patted his arm. "Now get over to that table and let's get some vittles in you. You're looking much too thin, my boy."

Pulling off his muddy boots, and dropping his haversack, Gabriel did as ordered; though, if anyone looked too thin, she did.

"How long can you stay?"

He took hold on the closest chair to pull it out. "Almost three days. 'Til Christm—"

The door burst open with a gust of winter air. "I came as soon as I heard about..."

Fugitive blonde locks clung to the young woman's reddened cheeks. She stared at him, mouth agape. "Gabe?"

He fought the urge to sink into the chair. "Clara."

Still as beautiful as ever—even more so than the image his memory had clutched the past three years.

The moisture pooling over her azure irises blinked away as her gaze dropped to his uniform. Her eyes narrowed. "You need to leave."

Gabriel forced a laugh. "You aren't the one who decides that. What are you doing here, anyway?"

Clara twisted and pushed the door closed, cutting off the draft. "I have more right to be here than you." Her chin jutted upward as she turned back. "Lawrence and I are engaged."

"You and Larry? But—"

"You left." She held her palm up to him. "I'm not here to reminisce with you, Gabriel. In fact, I should keep my mouth closed and let our soldiers find you. Better yet, I should tell them you're here so they can drag you out and give you the whipping you deserve."

Fire lit the ends of his nerves. So much for any affection she'd had for him. "You know they wouldn't stop there. After they got done beating me within an inch of my life, they would put a bullet between my eyes. Now, what Confederate soldiers? Why are they coming here?"

Clara's eyes darted between Gabriel and his mother. "Pa stopped by the farm to check on us... and to let me know that Lawrence has been hurt."

His stomach formed a large knot as he stole a glance at his mother. Her palm pressed over her mouth. *Not Larry, too, Lord.* He looked back to Clara. "How bad?"

"I don't know. But he's being brought here. I thought they'd come by now."

The whinny of a horse cut through the solid walls. His mother gripped his arm. "They can't find you, Gabriel."

After two steps, he pulled up the curtain in the window just enough to see through the snow to the party of three or four men and a wagon only ten yards up the road. Too late to try slipping out the front. Trapped.

"In the loft, son." She motioned him toward steep steps beside the bedroom door.

He gave a nod and squeezed her shoulder. "I'm sorry, Mama."

He shouldn't have come. Shouldn't have endangered her, too. Scrambling up the stairs, he dove over the small bed that had served him as a youth, and pulled part of the patchwork quilt over his body. He'd grown a mite and he had to bend his knees to hide his feet… His feet. His boots remained near the door. And his haversack.

Below him, the hinges sang.

Clara's heart thudded against her ribs, just as it had been doing since she'd walked in and found Gabriel here. As much as she hated the dark blue uniform he wore, she couldn't deny how striking he looked. Especially his equally blue eyes. She laid a hand against her stomach. She had no time for the fluttering or the churning as a knock sounded at the door.

"Come in." Martha Morgan's voice cracked.

A soldier in grey hurried inside, stomping his shoes to knock the mud from them. Clara choked back a gasp. Gabriel's tall black boots stood not two feet from the Confederate soldier. She wiped her moist palms across the sides of her skirt and attempted to keep her eyes averted from them and the military pack. Would they be recognizable as Union issue? Either way, they could raise questions about their owner.

The soldier addressed Martha. "Madam, we have brought your son, Private Morgan. He has a shoulder wound but there is nothing more the surgeon can do for him and there are too many other men to care for. Since you lived so near, we thought it best to bring him here. Where would you like him laid?"

Clara looked from the soldier to Martha. The poor woman's face had lost all color. "Why don't I draw back the covers on the bed? That's probably the best place for him." She waved the soldier out of the door. "You go help bring him in."

No sooner than the man turned his back, Clara snatched up Gabriel's boots and pack. Holding them low so her skirts would shield them, she hurried into the bedroom and shoved them under the bed. She drew back the quilts as the soldiers trudged across the floor and heaved Lawrence onto the thin mattress. Her hand stole to her mouth. His right shoulder and most of his chest had been wrapped in bandages stained crimson, brighter shades of scarlet still seeping from the center.

As the soldiers left, Clara moved to his head and ran her fingers across his ashen brow, wet with sweat.

"Oh, Lawrence." Martha fell to her knees at the side of the bed. She grasped her son's hand. "Lord, please save my boy. Please… Oh, please."

Clara blinked but only dislodged the moisture blurring her vision. Droplets rolled down her cheeks as a motion drew her gaze to the bedroom doorway. Gabriel's large frame and blue coat filled it as he stepped through. The heavy trod of hooves and the squeak of an axle confirmed the Confederates' departure. She glowered at him. "Look what you've done."

He stopped. "How am I responsible for this?"

"You're one of *them*." She clamped her eyelids closed against the pain etching itself into his handsome features.

Lawrence groaned then coughed, and Clara pivoted to him. She glanced into his brown eyes, then to his mother's. Martha leaned over, hope lighting her face. "Lawrence?"

His voice came as a hoarse rumble from the back of his throat. "Mama?"

"I'm here, love. And Clara." She brushed her thumb across his face, darkened with dirt and smoke. "Even Gabriel's come back to us. We're finally together again."

His brow pressed together with confusion, and then a scowl. "Gabe?"

Gabriel hastened to stand behind Martha. He reached for his brother's arm, but Lawrence jerked it away, wincing from the pain of the movement. "Stay away from me." His lip curled as he stared at his older brother. "Somebody, make him go away. I don't want him here."

"But, Larry." Gabriel's eyes widened with pleading.

"Get him out!"

Clara hurried around the bed and grabbed Gabriel's arm. She tugged him toward the door. "The least you can do is respect his wishes."

Gabriel's gaze remained on his brother as he retreated from the room. His fingers tangled themselves in her sleeve. "Tell me something I can do for him. What does he need?"

"He needs you to stay away." She swatted his hand. "You don't belong here anymore. Go back to your army, Gabe."

Not able to meet his gaze, Clara pushed the bedroom door closed. She leaned into the solid wood, the hurt on Gabriel's face wringing her heart.

Gabriel stared into the blackness of the loft, his feet hanging over the end of his bed. The last twenty-four hours, since he walked in that door, seemed cloaked in a strange sort of haze. Much like clouds of smoke wafting over a battlefield. The murmur of his mother's voice tightened his chest. With sleep eluding him, he rolled to his feet, pulled on his trousers and crept to the head of the stairs. Now that Clara was gone, maybe if Lawrence slept, he'd be allowed to sit with him.

The flickering from the fireplace danced across the wall, the only light. Mama stood at the table, her hands braced against it, her head bowed. "I do not know Thy plans for my boys. I cannot keep them here or safe. I cannot even be sure my baby boy will survive the night." Her shoulders trembled. "One more Christmas, Lord. One more Christmas as a family, with love and peace at this hearthside. And forgiveness. Just one more Christmas. All I ask."

He shifted and the stairs squeaked beneath him. Her hands wiped across her face as she turned. "What are you doing awake?"

Gabriel motioned to the bedroom door. "Am I supposed to be able to sleep? How's he doing?"

Weariness strained her voice. "The bleeding has stopped again. He's in a lot of pain, but seems to be resting all right." She slipped into the nearest chair. "What about you?"

His gaze dropped to the bottom stairs as he found a seat on them. "It hardly matters."

"It does to me."

He pushed the air from his lungs. "Numb." That about summed it up. "Somehow, I pictured Pa still sitting there in his chair by the fireplace reading his Bible or cleaning that old musket Grandpa used during the Revolution. I hoped to make my peace with him." He pressed his thumb and forefinger into his temples. "Then, to see Larry all... and him hating me. And Clara. She was angry when I left, but I still held out hope that after the war..." Everything that really mattered in his life was broken up—much like he was inside. But Mama had enough to worry about, so he straightened his spine and heaved himself to his feet. "I'm all right. I'd like to sit with Lawrence awhile, if I can."

"Of course, though Clara's still with him."

He glanced at the door beside him. Great. "I thought I heard her leave hours ago."

"Her mother came to see if there was anything she needed. You probably heard her."

"I recognized the voice. Just assumed they went home together. Clara's been in there for a full day. Can't you tell her to go home?"

Mama raised a brow. "Why don't you?"

Gabriel pulled his palm over the week-old beard clinging to his jaw then squared off to the door. "I think I will."

A candle on the bedside table cast a gentle glow over Lawrence's sleeping form and lit the delicate contours of Clara's face. Her elbows rested on her knees, her hands clasped. She looked up. "What are you doing here?"

He moved to her and wrapped his fingers around her elbow. "It's my turn to sit with him. Lawrence may be your fiancé, but he's my brother."

Standing, Clara folded her arms across her abdomen. "He doesn't want you here."

"That's between him and me." Gabriel reclaimed her arm and directed her to the door. "I'll leave when he asks me to."

Her feet slid to a halt as she twisted to him. Her mouth opened, probably with another retort, but no words came. Instead, she stared, her gaze moving between his eyes and his lips. Did she remember their kisses as fondly as he? His hand glided up her arm, touched the curve of her ear, the slope of her jaw. "How long did it take you to forget me?"

Her chin trembled and she tilted her face away.

"Why my brother?"

She looked at him, but not in the eyes. "I care deeply for Lawrence. And he's not as foolhardy as you."

"Granted. But do you love him—like you loved me?"

"Leave me alone, Gabriel. You left, remember?"

Yes. How could he forget? "Clara, I'm so sorry."

"Sorry for what, exactly? You're still wearing that uniform."

He swallowed hard, but it did little to dislodge the lump expanding in his throat. "I'm sorry for hurting you. I'm sorry I disappointed you."

"But not at all sorry that you turned your back on your community, your family. Tell Lawrence how sorry you are, Gabriel. Tell your Pa."

Her words plowed into his chest and he staggered back a step.

"It's too late for apologies." She twisted on her heel and yanked the door closed between them.

Clara clamped her hand over her mouth to block the sound of her sobs. She sagged against the closest wall. The memory of the agony in his blue eyes shredded her insides. And she'd been the one to inflict it. Why his brother? Yes, she cared for Lawrence, loved him even, but mostly their engagement had been a way to pretend Gabriel didn't exist anymore. She was pretty sure Lawrence felt the same way. Gabriel had abandoned them both, and they had exacted their revenge.

Success.

Across the room, Martha reclined in the rocking chair, the slow sway revealing that she was awake and had heard every word spoken.

Clara hurried to pull her shoes on, and her woolen cape.

"It's too late to walk home by yourself." Thankfully, Martha kept her eyes on the fire. "Why don't you go lay down in the loft?"

Where Gabriel had been sleeping? No. She had to distance herself from him. Clara made a beeline to the door.

"I'll return in the morning," she called over her shoulder before plunging into the cold night air. Again, white crystals floated down, every one of them melting as soon as they touched the earth, only deepening the mud that clung to her soles as she made her way back to town, passing the small church. High in the base of the steeple, a single brass bell hung silent. Almost four years into this war, no songs or merriment met the wee hours of Christmas Eve.

Gabriel's consciousness drifted. With his head tipped back and arms folded, the hours of the night passed in slow procession. Lawrence slept restlessly, but he slept. Hopefully a good sign. The thought of losing his little brother, too... Could he bear it?

Gabriel forced his aching eyes open to the show of dawn behind the pale blue fabric draped across the window. He stood and drew the curtain. Only one full day remained until he needed to start back to rejoin to his regiment. One day until Christmas. He looked to his brother. If only there were a way to give Mama her wish.

He dropped back into the chair and raked his fingers through his hair.

"Why are you here?"

The gravelly voice brought his head up. His brother watched him. "I wanted to make sure you and Mama were all right."

A muscle twitched in Lawrence's cheek. "Well, now you know. You can leave... *again.*"

Gabriel reached for the water pitcher. "Do you want a drink?"

"I don't want anything from you. How did you even get here dressed like a Yank?" Understanding lit Lawrence's eyes. His teeth ground together. "You fought with them at Marion, didn't you?"

Gabriel glanced away.

"And Saltville?"

"Yes." The word scratched his throat. His forced himself to look to his brother's tortured expression. "You, too?"

Lawrence nodded his head toward his bandaged shoulder. "Where do you think I got this? That second day, near the saltworks."

Gabriel slumped into the chair. For all he knew, one of his shells had almost killed his own brother. "You know, I never pictured fighting here."

"Does it matter? They killed Pa in Pennsylvania."

"Mama told me you were there, too."

Lawrence closed his eyes and relaxed into the pillow. Pain pinched the corners of his mouth. "I joined up in June. That was the first time I'd seen a real battle, never mind been in the thick of one. But I loaded my gun and aimed straight... just like my brother taught me. All them lines of blue coats. Couldn't stop wondering if he was one."

"I reckon that helped with your aim."

His eyes flashed open, and he glared. "I can't say."

Gabriel stood and walked to the door. "I'll tell Mama you're awake. And don't worry, I won't be here much longer."

Clara's head jerked up as Gabriel plunked a scraggly spruce just inside the door of the bedroom. "What is that?"

He flashed a grin as he knelt to tack a makeshift stand onto the trunk. "Surely you've seen a Christmas tree before."

"Yes, but it looked nothing like that."

"Don't be so quick to judge. There's potential." He glanced at his brother. "Remember that year Pa was away? We didn't want to wait, so we went out ourselves. You must have been six or seven, and me maybe ten. I still remember the look on Mama's face."

Probably because you saw it again when you hauled this tree past her. Clara bit her tongue.

With no reply from Lawrence, Gabriel stood the tree upright and left. A few minutes later, he returned with a handful of nuts, a single candle, some string and clusters of crimson berries that he began to distribute amongst the branches.

"Are those rosehips?"

"We needed something to brighten this room."

Try as she might, Clara found it impossible not to watch him as he adorned the tree, humming a familiar tune. No longer wearing Yankee blue, his old homespun shirt fit snug across his back, stressing at the seams. He'd grown into quite the man in his absence. She glanced to Lawrence to find his gaze on her. Warmth crept to her cheeks. "I'll go help your mama with dinner."

The noonday sun filtered through the windows, and logs crackled in the hearth. Gabriel's song followed her. *Hark the herald angels sing, glory to the newborn King.* Who was he trying to fool? Did he really believe he could pretend he'd never left, or expect the same of them?

She wiped her palms across her full skirts as she joined Martha at the table. One arm cradled a large wooden bowl, while the other wielded a spoon. A hint of ginger and cinnamon teased her senses. "What are you making?"

"A gingerbread loaf for the boys. I wanted to do something special for Christmas." Her eyes glistened. "You saw that tree Gabriel dragged through here."

"Yes, poor thing."

Martha shrugged. "He didn't dare to go too far looking for one. Besides, it's much better than we've had in years. The last couple…" She sighed. "I don't want to think about those other Christmases. I only have one day."

One day. "What can I do to help?"

Martha smiled at her. "My request is probably not what you have in mind, but Gabriel's humming has that hymn running through my mind and I have always considered your voice so very pretty."

Clara stared. "You want me to sing?"

"Christmas carols."

Throat constricting, she stepped to the nearest chair, bracing against its tall back. The words, and even the exuberance came easier than expected. "Hark the herald angels sing, 'Glory to the newborn King. Peace on earth and mercy mild, God and sinners reconciled.'"

"Joyful, all ye nations rise." A smooth baritone joined her, entering the room. "Join the triumph of the skies. With th' angelic host proclaim: 'Christ is born in Bethlehem!'" Loud and strong, Gabriel's voice resonated within the walls of the house, filling it. Filling her. "Hark the herald angels sing, 'Glory to the newborn King!'"

"I'm sorry, Martha, I don't think this was a good idea."

Gabriel brushed past her on his way to the fireplace. He crouched and tossed another log onto the blaze, though it wasn't needed. "There is no harm in a little carol. I'm sure you can remember to hate me tomorrow."

"It's not that."

"I'll keep my mouth closed if it helps. I'm sure your fiancé enjoyed your singing." He stabbed the poker into the coals, sending up a spray of embers.

"Gabe."

He looked back with a solemn smile pressed on his lips. "I'm serious, Clara. Sing for Lawrence. I'm not trying to get in the way."

She blew out her breath. He didn't have to try. With the sound of his voice in her head, Clara cleared her throat and resumed the song. For Lawrence. For Martha. For one day.

Music, food, and even laughter, but though Martha and Gabriel did their best, none of it felt real. Nothing more than a charade.

Evening stretched itself over the valley, and the sun vanished away. Clara helped change the bandages on Lawrence's shoulder. Already the gaping wound appeared improved and his temperature was normal. No need for a constant vigil over his bed. After reading to him for a while, she pressed a kiss to his forehead. "You sleep and I'll see you in the morning."

He nodded, but said nothing. He'd been silent most of the day—ever since Gabriel brought in that ridiculous-looking Christmas tree. On her way to the door, she wet her fingers and pinched out the single candle perched near the top.

"Clara?"

She glanced back to Lawrence. "Yes?"

"I miss having a brother... Is that wrong?"

The ache in his voice tugged at her. "I don't know."

She stepped out and moved toward the table to set a cloth over the remaining slices of gingerbread. Martha again sat in the rocker, but this time there was no motion, only heavy breathing. The last two days had taxed her greatly.

Gabriel appeared to have retired, as well. Disappointment nagged, but it was for the best. Pulling her cape from a peg near the door, Clara wrapped it around her shoulders and stepped into the crisp air. Snow laid itself as a clean blanket over the ground and sparkled in the air. As though a chime in the wind, the church bell began to toll.

Christmas had arrived.

"Do you hear that?"

Clara startled at the rumble of the deep voice and spun to where Gabriel leaned against the wall. She laid her hand over her heart, willing it to return to a regular pace. "The bell?"

He nodded, still staring into the distance. "Peace on earth, good will to men."

"What?"

"Isn't that what they sing? Peace on earth?"

If only. "Not anymore. There's no peace to be had." Her gaze darted to him. "Or good will. Only hate. Pain. Death. War."

Gabriel shook his head, pushing away from the wall to face her fully. "You're wrong." His lips curved with a simple smile. "God lives."

Finding her hand, he raised her knuckles to his lips for a gentle kiss. "Merry Christmas, Clara."

He stepped around her and into the house.

"Gabe."

He glanced back. "I understand."

The door closed and she started for home, the bell's song fading to the silence of a winter's night. How could she not question God's existence… or at least His wakefulness?

Gabriel's fingers sped to button his coat. Then he smoothed his hands over the clean blue wool. His mother's unconditional love still left him dazed. He would forever thank God for it. And for this Christmas. Not everything Mama had prayed for, but he'd done his best. Maybe next year would bring the war to an end and wounds could begin to heal.

After descending the stairs three at a time, Gabriel paused before entering his parents' bedroom. He straightened his uniform, though perhaps it would have been better to say his goodbyes before donning it.

Pillows propped up Lawrence's head, and his face held more color than yesterday. Good to see. His eyes flickered to Gabriel's, and then lowered to stare at the uniform.

"You take care of yourself and finish healing. God willing, the war will be over soon."

No acknowledgement whatsoever. But what could be expected?

Heart squeezing, Gabriel turned to his mother and wrapped her in his arms. "Thank you, Mama."

She kissed his cheek, then pressed it to hers. "Thank you for coming home. I won't stop praying that the Good Lord will continue to watch over you."

He managed a nod, and looked to Clara. She met his gaze, but said nothing.

"Goodbye." Gabriel made a hasty withdrawal. No use letting everyone see him cry.

Clara stared at the door even after Gabriel was gone, pressure building behind her eyes. How long could she contain it?

"You're still in love with him, aren't you?"

She glanced at Lawrence and a smile touched his mouth.

Tears spilled. "I'm afraid I am."

The muscles danced in his cheeks. "Then tell him."

"What?"

He sniffed and extended his good hand to his mother. She took it, her eyes wide. He looked to Clara. "And tell him I said to take care of himself. Tell him we'll be waiting for him to come home again."

She remained in place, her mind spinning, her heart leaping.

"It'll be too late if you don't hurry."

Clara staggered to her feet and through the house. The glare of the morning sun, brilliant off the white ground, blinded her. Boot tracks marked Gabriel's path around the house and into the orchard. Grabbing her skirts almost to her knees, she raced across the yard toward the blue clad figure. "Gabe!"

He turned.

Her face was dry and her breath gone by the time she caught up. She gripped his sleeve. "I… I hear the bells."

Questioning ridged his brow but before he could speak, she kissed his mouth.

"I finally hear the bells. Lawrence does, as well. Peace on earth, good will to men. Faith. Hope." A smile tugged at the corners of her lips as more tears tumbled free. "Love."

"And forgiveness, Clara?"

She touched his face and pushed up on her toes to again find his mouth. His arms encircled her, drawing her against him as he kissed her in return. Long and deep, the taste of salt on his lips.

Clara smoothed a tear from his cheek, her gaze holding his. "Merry Christmas to you, too, Lieutenant Gabe Morgan. You come back to us, you hear?"

About the Author: Angela K. Couch

Angela K. Couch is an award-winning author for her short stories, and a semi-finalist in ACFW's 2015 Genesis Contest. Her childhood was spent listening to her father read chapters from his novels, and Angela decided young to follow his path. A passionate believer in Christ, her faith permeates the stories she tells. Her martial arts training, experience with horses, and appreciation for good romance sneak in there, as well. Angela lives in Alberta, Canada, with her "hero" and three munchkins.

Visit her at http://www.angelakcouch.com

The Missing Piece

by Kathleen Neely
(Second Place)

I don't know why I agreed to do this. The last thing I wanted to do on a Saturday morning was go to a yard sale and look through someone else's rejects. Oh, wait. Marti reminded me that it's an estate sale, as if that made it more prestigious. Well, as far as I was concerned, yard sale, garage sale, estate sale—it was still junk. Puzzles, dishes, games, all with missing pieces. I really didn't want to go. I didn't need to save a buck by wearing someone else's stains or reading their dog-eared books. But Marti could wear a person down. She planned to equip her apartment with shabby-chic hand-me-downs. I was the last person in the world to help with that. And less than a week before Thanksgiving? Bad timing.

Pulling on my new designer straight-leg jeans, my luxury leather boots, and topping it all with a pillow-soft suede jacket, I stole a glance in the mirror. I'd absolutely not go looking like I needed to shop hand-me-downs.

A series of loud honks from Marti's little hatchback told me that she was in my driveway, impatiently waiting. I wouldn't allow her to hurry me. It was eight in the morning, for goodness sakes! I would have elected to go at noon.

We arrived at a neighborhood that served a mature community, a euphemism for old people. I groaned at the pedestrians flocking toward the driveway, and at the cars lining both sides of the narrow street. It looked like a blue light special at a discount store. Inching ahead with the crowd, we arrived in the first room open to the public. It would have been the dining room if furniture had been left to define it. Instead, white folding tables filled both sides of the walls with an assortment of junk. One side had stacks and stacks of linens. How many people lived here anyway? They were neatly folded and so crisp that I could swear I felt starch. I ran my fingers along the faded flowers on the pilled fabric of a queen-sized sheet. The elastic corner disclosed evidence that it had been fitted and laundered many times over. No thank you. I prefer Egyptian cotton at 500 threads.

The sun shone through the window and reflected off a box of old, glass Christmas ornaments, sending a colorful prism to rest on the wall. Maybe, by some miracle, I would find an antique artifact for my tree. Once I was able to squeeze my way across the room, I peered into the box and had to stifle a laugh. Atop some vibrantly colored pieces of broken glass rested ornaments, none without significant defects, scratches, chips, and missing parts. Beside the box of mishap decorations was a bag of tangled tree lights, an elf minus one pointy ear, and a shiny silver garland. Clearly, I'd be leaving empty handed.

Marti had moved to a different room, so I pushed through the maze of people to look for her. I peeked into the area cordoned off with yellow tape; surely all of the good stuff remained behind those barriers. Craning my head, I peeked at the furniture stacked against one wall and boxes packed for who knew where. It couldn't all go to the old folks' home. Perhaps there were grown children quibbling over the decent possessions.

Three rooms later, I caught sight of Marti with her arms full. When she saw me, relief and worry merged in her expression. The worry had better not mean she was short of funds for the load of castoffs in her hoarding hands.

"Sandra, hurry over here. You've got to see this." She led me to an area near the checkout table and lowered her stash to the floor, searching for something amid the mess. She had managed to commandeer a box filled with stained coffee mugs, a skillet with thread-thin lines etched into a non-stick finish, and at least a half-dozen picture frames of varied sizes and styles, some still containing pictures.

Marti's hands shoveled to the item she wanted to show me. She turned it toward me with a questioning look. The gilded frame housed a 5x7 photograph, dusty from neglect. A small diagonal crack splintered the glass in the upper right corner. Not a sale item that would draw anyone else's attention, yet the blood drained from my face and traveled the path to my stomach.

I opened my mouth to speak, but my lips made silent gestures. The air was suddenly in short supply, but I managed to whisper, "Buy the picture. I'm going to the car."

We drove home in silence, Marti frowning in disappointment. I shushed her about the question fresh on her lips. "I don't know, Marti. Just let me think."

My tone left no opening for discussion. With muddled thoughts, I needed to look at the picture again, but it was crammed in the box deep in the rear of the hatchback.

Once I was alone and seated at my dining room table, I stared into the photograph. I could have been looking into a cracked, gilt-framed mirror. The washed-out strawberry blond of my hair, the slight upturn of the tip of my nose, the same flecks of freckles that I hated and covered with the help of expensive cosmetics. There was intensity in the eyes, revealing a strong personality like the one I possessed. The features were mine. But I never had hair pulled back and tied into a pony tail. I never owned, nor would I, a faded lavender shirtdress tired from overuse.

Who was the other woman in the picture? In her late forties, early fifties, her arm lay casually draped across the shoulder of the girl that was my double. In the background, there was a small, fenced pasture at the base of a rocky cliff. Grass climbed the fence posts peeling with some degree of neglect. The woman was looking at the girl, not at the camera, and her profile featured a tender smile. The affectionate gaze took the attention off herself, deflecting to the girl who was clearly the focal point.

What did this mean? Did everyone really have a twin somewhere? My mind raced to formulate a logical answer.

I pulled out a photograph that was taken four years ago, on my 21st birthday, and held them side-by-side. Looking slender in a sleeveless black dress, sleek and shimmering, even I had to admit that it revealed too much endowment. I wore five-inch heels that had caused blisters that I hid for the following two weeks. The girl in the photo wore practical, flat loafers. I wore what I thought at the time was a sophisticated expression. She wore contentment, a softer countenance that appeared so genuine. Why did I suddenly feel like I didn't measure up?

After entertaining every possibility that I could, tears stung my eyes. Could I have a twin? My parents were very open about my adoption, and I thought I knew all of the circumstances. There was never mention of a sibling. Surely they wouldn't separate twins.

I must talk with my mother. The gilded picture and I would make the hour and a half drive to my parent's house.

Christmas was a big deal in our neighborhood. There was always a 'best decorated award' given by the homeowners' association, and people battled for it. I found my mother seated on the floor amid tangled outdoor lights, testing each string.

"Hi Sandra. I wasn't expecting you till Thanksgiving Day. Forgive me for not getting up, but I'm on a roll here."

I wasn't planning to join her on the floor. My mind was too distracted to test light bulbs. "How long will you be? I need to talk about something."

"How important, scale of one to ten?"

That was her way of centering me. She always asked that with a smile, saying I treated every problem like a ten until I thought it through. Well, this could be a one, or it could be an eleven.

I rolled my eyes. "I don't know, Mom. Just tell me how long you'll be."

She slid the strings of lights from her lap and stood up. My mom had a classic refinement, beautiful even as she aged. It was easy to see that I was adopted: her raven hair and dark complexion a glaring contrast to mine.

"Tell me about my adoption."

Her eyebrows shot up, but she also smiled. "Well, I've told you before, but I'm always happy to talk about the most joyful time of my life."

"I just want to hear it again. With all details."

Mom recounted her disappointment when they were never able to conceive, the decision to adopt, the wait for a call, and the moment when they first saw me at three months old. I was not adopted at birth because my birthmother kept me until she died in a car accident. Paternity was unknown, and no other family members came forward. Nothing new in the details. I had heard it all before.

I reached into my bag, pulled out the photograph, and handed it to my mother. She looked at it for a while before speaking.

"Wow. That's a remarkable resemblance. Really remarkable."

"Could I have a twin?"

There was a long pause before she answered. "No, of course not. They would never separate twins." But that long pause proved she also had some doubts. "Remember that Facebook campaign, Twin Strangers? There were others with amazing look-alikes. I'm sure that is what this is."

"Yeah, but think about this. Those people were living far from each other. This is right in the same town. And the fact that I'm adopted throws in an element of possibility."

We were both silent. Her eyes looked sad when they met mine and that told me a lot. I made a decision. "I have to find her. I've got to know."

I stayed at my parents' home that night, sleeping in my childhood bed. With a lavish floral comforter embracing me, I sank into the welcoming solace. Was it my sister looking at me from the frame on my nightstand? Her satisfied smile softened the brilliance of the gray/green eyes. My eyes had always been one of my best assets. They spoke confidence, resilience, self-reliance. What did her eyes speak? They were incredible eyes, brilliant and drawing you into them, but they spoke gentleness, tenderness. I thought of Shakespeare's words, "The eyes are a window to the soul." I could not look away from them, until my own filled with tears, spilling and clouding my vision.

How did that happen? Me, a silver-spoon kid. I grew up with all of the amenities of life. My eyes should be contented and satisfied. Not hers, in her style-less clothing, leaning into the arm of an unpretentious middle-aged mom. I had to find her. I absolutely had to find her and learn the truth.

As I drifted off, I pictured faded floral sheets, threadbare and pilled, starched to a crisp coolness, my sister laying upon them, softly breathing the rhythm of sleep.

I decided to canvas the neighborhood where the estate sale had been held, carrying the picture house to house. Someone would have an idea whose photo was in the frame. One neighbor finally passed along a contact.

"Heddy will know, if anyone does. She and Gloria were real close. Real close." She explained that Gloria was the homeowner who had moved into assisted living. Gloria would be my last resort, since I didn't know if she was sick or frail.

I went to see Heddy, the very close friend. She volunteered at the Senior Center, and I was told I would find her there. She was among a room full of volunteers preparing for a Thanksgiving food basket distribution. Tables were loaded high with non-perishables. Heddy stopped her task of dividing canned goods and led me to a sitting area.

"Oh yes, Gloria and me go way back. Way back to when we was kids. Went to school together and lived across the street most of our lives. I told Gloria just about everything, and she did the same back. No secrets between us."

While I attempted to get to the point, Heddy was having a grand time reminiscing, informing me, in great detail, about the people who lived next to Gloria and those three doors down. She glanced at the picture in my hand, but seemed to sense that once it was addressed, she would lose her audience. But I could be persistent too.

"Heddy." I took her hand to express the importance of my next words. "This picture was with Gloria's estate sale. Do you know who these people are?"

She took the picture from my hand and gave me a knowing look, her gaze traveling from my hair to my eyes and examining the details of my face. "Sure do." She paused to give me one more scrutinizing glance. "This here is Gloria's niece, Evelyn, and Evelyn's daughter, Grace."

Grace. My unsteady hands reached for the picture. I needed to look at her and say the name. Grace.

"Heddy, do you know if Grace was adopted?"

"Oh, yes, honey. She was a true blessing to Evelyn when she found that she couldn't birth her own baby. Just two weeks old when they got her, and tiny. The tiniest little thing you ever saw."

Tears threatened to form in my eyes, but I refused them and feigned composure. My sister. My twin. It had to be. Adopted at two weeks. They tore her from me and left me alone for almost three more months. Did Evelyn not want me, or didn't she know I existed?

"Do you know when her birthday was?" My voice cracked with emotion despite my best efforts.

"Well, I know that it was somewhere 'round about Christmas time, a little before or after. Don't recollect the date, but I remember Gloria saying that she was just the sweetest little Christmas present."

December 21st. My birthday. Grace's birthday.

"Do you know where I can find Evelyn and Grace? Do you know their last name?"

Heddy looked sorrowful and cold washed over me, raising goose bumps. "Oh honey, that's the sad thing. You can find Evelyn in Union County where she is living, but little Grace, she went home early. Only twenty-one when the good Lord called her. Leukemia. Took her quick, once they found it."

We shared a womb, then never saw each other again. A moan escaped, and my shaking hand attempted to cover it. I tried to stand, but my uncooperative legs swayed. Heddy took my hand and pulled me back to my seat. "You sure do remind me of that girl."

With Thanksgiving just two days away, I had to wait until the following week before contacting Evelyn. I called first so she wouldn't think she was seeing a ghost. She agreed to see me, despite the doubt in her voice.

The little town was rural, with small homes set at the end of long gravel driveways. White Christmas lights gave it a surreal, postcard appearance. Nothing flashy or prominent, just a calm, unhurried feel.

As I turned into the driveway that my GPS identified, I scanned my clothing. I shouldn't have chosen the classy monogramed blazer and cashmere scarf. I striped off both and slid a simple nylon jacket over my turtleneck.

The lady answering my knock was definitely the same one in the photo, although the extra years had aged her face. When the porch light illuminated my features, she gasped, her hand flying to her heart. "Oh my."

"Evelyn?"

"Yes, yes. Please come in."

A four-foot tall Christmas tree glowed in the corner, sending an aroma of pine throughout the room.

"Please sit." She gestured to a living room armchair.

How many times had my sister sat in this very space? My eyes filled with tears before I had a chance to speak. Evelyn rushed to my side and perched on the arm of the chair.

"Oh, child. I didn't know. They never told me. I would've had you both."

My tears were flowing freely now. "Why would they do that?"

"I don't know. Things were different then, and it was a small agency."

She got over the shock of seeing my face, and I got past the awareness that I was in the space where my sister had lived. I stayed longer than I had planned, talking and watching old VHS movies.

Evelyn and I laughed as Grace, at seven, tended the horses, clumsily carrying a bucket of feed. Grace, at ten, bringing in a bunch of hand-picked daisies, her favorite flower. We smiled, watching Grace as a young adult volunteering in the Children's Home — a place for children whose parents couldn't care for them. When we came to the video where Grace had lost so much weight and her head was adorned with a scarf, I carried the tissues and joined Evelyn on the sofa. She placed her arm around my shoulder as it had been around Grace's in the picture.

"December must be so hard for you with both her birthday and Christmas."

"Oh, we miss her every day. But, yes, her absence is felt when Christmas comes. Would you like to see a picture of Grace's last Christmas?" She didn't wait for my answer, but pulled a photo book from a shelf. "Tell me if you see anything unusual here."

The picture showed Grace seated on a stool near the tree, hanging ornaments on the low branches. She was surrounded by colorfully wrapped gifts. The gauntness of her cheeks and the gray pallor evidenced the progression of her cancer. Still, she wore a smile that reached the hollow places of her face. She looked happy.

"Well, you can tell that she's really sick, but she still looks happy."

"You're right, but look harder. Anything else that jumps out at you?"

I examined the picture, and it suddenly hit me. "It's summer. The trees outside the window are green, and there are flowers all around them."

Evelyn smiled. "Grace never asked for much, but she wanted one more Christmas. We knew she wouldn't make it until December, so we just moved Christmas up."

"That's really special. I'm sure she was thankful."

"Well, more than that, it brought her hope."

What? I guess I looked perplexed because Evelyn continued.

"You see, Grace said that her journey with cancer was like the trip to Bethlehem. It looked like the worst of all plans, but God was up to something. We had reason to be discouraged, disappointed, and afraid, just like the people involved in Jesus' birth. But God was orchestrating everything to create a miracle.

"Think about it. Mary's parents surely had some doubts about their daughter's unbelievable story, and they had to endure the whole town whispering about her. Joseph had to make a decision about whether or not to believe her. He, too, would have been scorned by his friends. And Mary, well she faced the possibility of being stoned to death.

"Finally, when enough time had passed that things might have settled down a little bit at home, they were called to take a long trip. The Bible isn't clear on how they traveled, but it would've been on foot or with a donkey. Mary was very close to delivering her baby and had to travel eighty miles. No doctor. No hotels along the way, just camping on the ground. Think about how uncomfortable that had to be.

"And the wise men? God called them to see the child. They were far away and took months from their homes and families. Shepherds were poor men, and sheep were their livelihood. When the angels called them to the manger in Bethlehem, their sheep would have scattered and could have been harmed.

"The point is, this looks like the worst possible plan ever. But look how God brought all of those things together for the most incredible joy. A joy so great that we still celebrate it today. Grace said that just like them, we have our share of discouragement, disappointment, and fear. Christmas brought her hope because she knew that, despite what looked like the worst possible plan, God was planning for an incredible miracle.

"So, here is our August Christmas tree. It stayed up until September, when Grace saw the journey through. We grieved for us, but we rejoiced for her."

Grace's eyes. Her eyes were gentle, contented, peaceful—a window to her soul. Looking into them made me aware something was missing inside of me. Was it God that brought my sister her tenderness? Was there any tenderness inside of me? Surely there must be. She was my twin.

When I first saw Grace in her ordinary lavender dress and loafers, with the peeling fence in the background, I felt the compelling need to rescue her from her ordinary existence, to bring her into my world of abundance. But maybe it wasn't she who needed to be rescued.

The doorbell chimed and I opened my mother's massive front door, her lighted Christmas wreath casting a soft glow into the entry. Evelyn hugged me, and I introduced her to my parents. Today was our birthday, mine and Grace's. I turned twenty-five just three weeks after I learned that I had a sister.

We cut the cake and Evelyn shared stories about Grace's childhood while Mom and Dad shared about mine. The laughter was healthy. Gifts were waiting to be opened, then we would take flowers to the cemetery for Grace.

I still had selective taste, and my parents' gifts reflected that. What did Evelyn think as she witnessed our opulent lifestyle? Something gnawed inside me, uncomfortable with the extravagance that I had once savored. I didn't want Evelyn to feel that the gift she held in her lap was insignificant in comparison.

Evelyn looked at me with the same tenderness that she had for Grace. "Sandra, this is for you. Grace would have loved you so, and I'm sure she would want you to have these."

She held out a small box wrapped in white paper, with yellow ribbon with a daisy woven through it. I slid the daisy out and pressed the soft silkiness to my cheek, breathing deeply. I longed to have something of my sister—a touch, a scent, something. Sliding the daisy into my hair, I opened the box.

I had resisted the estate sale because I didn't want someone else's dog-eared books. Yet the precious books in the box were tattered from use. Grace's journals. I would actually hear her speak, her voice in writing, her thoughts, feelings, beliefs. She had captured them in words that would outlive her. I could barely stand the wait until I was alone in my bedroom tonight. Well, almost alone. Just me and my sister.

I ask myself the question - do you believe what you say you believe? I believe in heaven, in a perfect place where my blood will not have this poison coursing through it. Where I won't have pain racking my spine, and where I will have energy again. I covet that. So why do I hold on to this world for dear life? Do I believe what I say I believe? If so, I should be anxious to be there, in that perfect place where I'll be face to face with Jesus.

Yet I leave this world without ever filling that empty place that has been my constant companion. That "something missing" that I can never identify. Perhaps it does not exist on this side of heaven.

But I digress. I began today's entry determined to hold fast to thankfulness. Twenty-one blessed years with the joy of my family and the people that God has placed in my life. Blessed that I learned that true happiness is found in God alone. So I am thankful for my twenty-one years. And I am ready. I will loosen my grip, and perhaps I will find my missing piece.

Grace

About the Author: Kathleen Neely

 Kathleen Neely is a retired educator, wife, mother, and grandmother. After teaching elementary school, she moved into administration and worked as an elementary principal for Eden Christian Academy in Pittsburgh, PA, and for Shannon Forest Christian School in Greenville, SC. She is a member of ACFW and Cross N Pens, a local writing group. Her desire is to write wholesome fiction that honors Christ. A favorite scripture is Zephaniah 3:17--The Lord your God is in your midst, a mighty one who will save. He will rejoice over you with gladness, he will quiet you by his love, he will exalt over you with singing. (ESV) "How awesome is that!"

Twitter @NeelyKneely3628
kathyneely@gmail.com
Amazon.com/author/kathleenneely

Returning Christmas

by Emily Conrad
(Third Place)

With dark hair, green sweater and a toned build, he was Santa's opposite in every way. With one exception. As he made his way around the glittering ballroom, he doled out gifts from a large sack.

He would have no gift for her, so Gwen lowered her eyes to spare them both embarrassment. She'd only recently signed away an absurd portion of her paycheck for a lease and hadn't met any of her neighbors before the party began. Even an hour into it, she'd done little more than brush shoulders with the other tenants as she wandered the room. She never should've come to the Christmas party.

"Gwendolyn." Instead of rushing through the three syllables of her name, the man's warm voice fully pronounced each one as if he had all the time in the world for her.

Her eyes ticked to his face. Had he learned her name off the intercom by the front door? Friends called her Gwen, but she wouldn't correct him. In his mouth, her full name rang with a richness that suggested, however incorrectly, that she fit in among the poised and well-to-do neighbors.

He squeezed her hand. "I'm Maddox. Seven twenty-four."

When he released her hand to dig around in his bag, Gwen swirled her champagne glass. Alcohol never had much draw for her, but she'd needed something to hold on to.

"Four twenty-eight."

The ovals of a hundred other tenants' faces turned her direction, some more blatantly watching Maddox than others.

She forced her shoulders down and back and fidgeted to find a grip on the champagne glass that would lead her neighbors to believe she'd spent most her life socializing at fancy parties. "I chose it for the view of the bridge."

"The bridge?" He paused his rummaging and aimed his raised eyebrows her way. "Isn't your side of the building petitioning to tear that down?"

Gwen's face burned. She should never have come. Her paycheck earned her the space, but she would never fit in here. She shrugged. "It makes me think of London."

"One man's trash is another man's treasure. And speaking of treasures"—with a flourish, he presented a small box wrapped in gold paper—"I hope you find this to be one of them."

She waited. Surely he'd retract it, a cruel joke on the new, mousy tenant. But he didn't. "What did I do to deserve this?"

"It's not about deserving. It's a gift."

"You shouldn't have." And she meant it.

"But I did." He held the package ever closer, and she had no choice but to take it.

Gwen glanced around for a place to set the drink. A table stood a few feet away, circular and covered with a heavy tablecloth. How could he afford a gift for everyone? It had better be something silly, cheap. She'd just spent hundreds on gifts for her family. That, coupled with rent and other bills, had her bank account sulking. No extra remained to buy a gift in return for this, whatever it was. She stepped toward the table to free her hands, but Maddox signaled her to stop.

"Not here."

A couple entered the room, and he excused himself to trade gifts with them, leaving Gwen to study her present. As she turned the box, the curls of the bow tumbled over her fingers and drooped toward the floor. The wrapping was so beautiful that the gift inside must be… Must be something he hadn't meant to give to her. Surely, he'd come and ask for it back.

"I see you've been gifted."

Gwen looked up.

The speaker, a woman in black, nodded at the box in Gwen's hand. "Since you're a woman, it'll be the customary diamond necklace."

Gwen's mouth gaped and her shoulders hopped up and stiffened.

The woman rolled her eyes. "Maddox will give them to anyone, won't he?" She shook her head with something like disgust. Then she smiled slyly, refocusing her large eyes on Gwen. "Next year, it'll be about the same, value-wise." Gwen's older brother had once used the same tone to convince her a monster lived under her bed. "The following year depends."

She waited, but the woman remained silent.

"Depends on what?"

"On what you give him. He gives you two years to get the hang of his formula. Once things get going, he doubles the value of the gift you gave him the previous year. A beautiful system." The woman cackled.

"I don't even know him." She turned to catch up and give the gift back.

"Someone did that once." The woman gripped her shoulder. "He left immediately and mailed the rest of our gifts. Mailed them. Delayed them for *days*."

Gwen spun back. The last thing she wanted was to give the tenants a reason to hate her. "What if I don't give him anything? Will he stop?"

The woman's face went slack. "I don't think anyone's ever tried that."

The woman's eyes drifted, and she lifted her chin and waved at a woman across the room.

She was losing the chance to finally meet a neighbor, so Gwen stepped a little closer. "I'm Gwen."

"Charlize. Nice meeting you." She sauntered away without giving Gwen another glance.

Gwen wandered the room until she managed to insert herself into conversation with a single man named Phil and a married couple, Rachel and Richard. They rolled their eyes at Gwen's encounter with Charlize.

"She thinks she's a queen because she runs the tenant association." Rachel waved her hand at the glitter of the party around them. "This is her handiwork."

But as she spoke, Rachel's eyes followed Maddox, who had finished trading gifts and was making his way toward the exit. As the door swung shut behind him, Rachel and the two men at the table picked up their belongings and stood.

Ten o'clock hadn't yet come and gone. Given the open bar, why weren't people staying until the alcohol ran out?

"It was nice to meet you, Gwen." Rachel clutched her designer bag.

Phil picked up his gift from the table. "You should come with us tomorrow."

Rachel glared at him.

"What's tomorrow?" Gwen bent to look for her purse on the floor. No rush to find it, since the no-name brand would do nothing to make friends here.

"We always go to the mall. Exchange the gifts."

Her chin jerked up. "Exchange the gifts?"

Phil shrugged and nodded.

"Don't judge us." Rachel's smooth manicure dug into the supple leather of her purse. "I happen to know someone this year is getting a pair of Jet Skis."

Gwen narrowed her eyes. What was the relevance?

"We return the gifts so we can use the money toward the gift we'll give Maddox next year." Richard's blunt explanation left Phil looking sheepish and Rachel seething.

Gwen sat back in her chair. If refusing the gifts saddened Maddox, returning them would likely enrage him. She smiled to the others, who waited for her decision. "I'll have to pass."

She moved the tablecloth aside and spotted her purse. By the time she stood with it in hand, Rachel and Richard were already a table away, headed for the door.

Phil stayed behind. "It's ridiculous, really. The cost of the gifts goes up and up. " He shook his head, and they started toward the door. "Rachel and Richard played the game, and they're in over their heads. She doesn't see it that way, but the only way they can afford to keep it up is by returning what he gives them."

"So what's the point? If they don't get to keep it..."

Phil opened the door for her. "She keeps some of the money." They crossed the hall, and he pressed the button to call the elevator. "The rest goes toward his next present. Every year, she gets a couple hundred to keep while she still gets to give huge gifts to Maddox, making her look like she has more money than she truly does. It does wonders for her status around the building."

The doors dinged and opened.

Gwen gave him a sideways glance as she pressed the button for her floor. "It sounds like you don't approve."

"Well..." He stuffed his hands in his pockets. "If he gives me something I don't like, I'll exchange it." The elevator stopped on his floor. "Anyway, Merry Christmas."

When she made it to her apartment, Gwen slid the ribbon from around the gift. After cutting the tape on the gold wrapping, she unfolded the paper and opened the box. Three diamonds dangled from a white-gold chain on a bed of black velvet. She pressed a hand on the dining room table for balance.

She couldn't keep this. Now that Maddox had delivered all his gifts, it would inconvenience no one for her to return this to him.

Maddox would be disappointed, but it was ridiculous, like Phil said. Someone going through life in such a ridiculous way was bound to be disappointed.

She would march up to 724 in the morning. She would knock and, when he opened the door, she would put the box in his hands and firmly tell him, "No, thank you."

A year later, Gwen checked her appearance six times before she left for the Christmas party. Her looks weren't the problem; in college she'd come to terms with being plain. Her nerves grew from the fact that she'd not bought anything for Maddox.

His three-diamond necklace glittered at her throat. Over the past year, it'd become one of her favorite possessions. Maddox's game was too expensive to play, but she was a good person. Didn't she deserve a nice gift once in a while? Wasn't it about time God sent her a little blessing?

Maybe, maybe not.

She'd upped the work she did in the community and at church, just in case.

After the demanding hours she put in at the job that earned her this wonderful apartment, she was spread thin with volunteering at soup kitchens and outreaches. But she loved coming home to this place, and she loved the sparkle of this necklace. Unfortunately, the apartment and necklace couldn't cure the bags under her eyes.

The sixth time she stood before the mirror, she touched the necklace, then lifted her chin and rode the elevator to the ballroom, armed with her stack of greeting cards.

The scene set by Charlize, the tenant association president and head of the Christmas party committee, dropped Gwen's chin back down and curved her posture. Extravagance marked the ballroom. Instead of a string trio, a small band played on the stage, and a man in a turquoise cummerbund sang into a mic. A pair of ice sculpture swans spread their wings over the buffet table. She gripped her cards tighter and crossed the room to join a cluster of her neighbors.

Conversation centered on how little snow had fallen this year. They nibbled on hors d'oeuvres.

The man from the fifth floor predicted a brown Christmas.

The woman from 206 argued it would mostly be a grey Christmas, since, after all, they lived in the city with little vegetation to turn brown.

A couple of them eyed the door, and the others followed suit. Conversation petered out. Maddox had yet to arrive. Gwen joined them in the vigil because Maddox was the sole neighbor in whose presence she felt comfortable.

On the other hand, he was also the only neighbor she might be about to offend.

At nine, Maddox arrived to a quiet room that burst into a party when the attendees spotted him.

Gwen's nerves danced until he approached. Then the jitters turned ugly and stabbed her lungs.

"Still enjoying the view of the bridge?" He held the gift sack over his shoulder casually, as if everyone walked around with matching loads.

Still recovering her breath, she nodded.

His eyes dropped to her neck, and he smiled, showing the start of crow's feet. Gwen touched the diamonds. Maybe she shouldn't have worn the necklace. What made her think she deserved it or that her charity work would matter one ounce to her neighbor?

He reached into his bag and gave her a present the size of a department store clothing box.

Gwen accepted the gift and offered a card from her stack. "Merry Christmas."

"Merry Christmas, Gwendolyn."

That night in her apartment, Gwen opened the wrapping to find a wool coat and a silk scarf. The perfect fit and colors made her turn twice in front of the mirror, but afterward, she returned the gift to the box.

Maddox would demand this back after he opened the card.

In mid-January, Gwen wore the coat for the first time. When she stepped into the elevator, Maddox waited there, also on his way down.

He smiled as if he didn't notice how red her face had become, though she could see her reflection in the mirror walls of the elevator and knew the color to be as striking as the coat was beautiful.

"I'm glad to see you wearing it. After your thank you note, I'd have to be suspicious if I saw you going out without it."

"Suspicious?"

"Some of the others send notes, too, believe it or not. And then the next day..." He stared at the wall. "Some people would exchange any gift for something they could earn or buy, or for something more convenient. They would return Christmas itself, if they could." He offered Gwen a regretful smile.

"No one would return Christmas. It's too much fun."

Maddox fastened his gaze to the wall, his tight smile in place. "You'd be surprised. They just don't know who to return it to — or what their refund would be."

Thankfully, the doors slid open to the lobby.

"You'll see." His voice followed her as she stepped onto the marble of the lobby. He might be insane.

May as well stay on his good side. "It's a beautiful coat."

He managed a genuine smile before she hurried away.

The following year, the invitation to the annual Christmas party announced a black tie dress code. Gwen found a gown at a thrift store, probably some teenager's homecoming attire. The ivory satin, when accompanied by the diamond necklace, would satisfy the requirements of the party.

Gwen clasped the chain around her neck and scooped up her cards. As compliant as she'd been to the dress code, the cards were an act of rebellion: Charlize had dubbed this gathering a "holiday" party, so Gwen made certain her cards said "Merry Christmas" instead of "Warm Wishes" or "Peace and Joy."

The elevator delivered her to the second floor where she met Heather, a friendly neighbor she'd convinced to accompany her to the party.

The women entered the ballroom and found Charlize had upgraded the decor to match the dress code. A large dance floor accompanied the band and the ice sculptures. Also, each of the chairs, which hadn't been shabby to start with, were covered with cloth and decorated by large, red bows tied behind the backs. Out the windows, cars cut through new, wet snow. The two women took a seat at a table.

"He sounds like a weirdo to me," Heather said.

The January conversation with Maddox in the elevator had been weird, but Gwen had seen him since, and he'd managed some absolutely sane small talk. Still, she couldn't explain him and wouldn't try.

It was for the best that she'd kept back her opinions because, when Maddox entered the ballroom, he'd brought with him yet another surprise. This year, all of his golden gifts matched in size and color.

Heather lifted her hand to shield her mouth while Maddox was still twenty feet off. "White tie is fancier than black tie, isn't it? He outdid Charlize."

Maddox wore a black tux, but his shirt, vest, and bowtie were all white. Gwen smiled. So she wasn't alone in undermining Charlize tonight.

As he stepped up to the table, Maddox greeted both women by name. He presented one gift to Heather, then one to Gwen. "I hope it's a treasure."

Gwen's smile broadened at the familiar line.

He wished them each a Merry Christmas and moved on.

Heather cocked an eyebrow. "So I'm guessing this isn't a necklace. I moved in a year too late. Unless you think it's something better?"

Gwen took one box in each hand. They seemed to be the same weight. Too big for jewelry, too small for clothing. A card nestled under the bow of Gwen's but not Heather's.

"Well, anyway..." Heather sipped her wine. "He really lit up when he saw you."

"It's not like that." Gwen fiddled with the card. If only she didn't have to wait until later to know what it said.

Gwen passed the time in conversation with Heather until Maddox neared the door to leave. The party-goers sat perched and ready to break up for the year, but Charlize, in her elaborate black gown, swept back into the room.

"A Bible?" Charlize's voice trilled like a piccolo. "A Bible?"

All conversation ceased, but the band continued to play. Gwen strained to hear Maddox's response over the music.

"The gifts I've given this year are the most valuable I have to give."

"Then you're either a liar or a lunatic. Perhaps both. Either way..."

A musician, perhaps distracted by the outburst, hit a renegade drum, and the sound popped through the ballroom. Maddox staggered like Rachel, who danced drunk in Richard's arms. Charlize had been right; he took refusals of his gifts hard.

Too hard. He dropped to his knees and braced a hand on the floor. The music stopped, and Gwen rose to her feet.

The pop hadn't been a drum. Charlize's hand hid in the folds of her gown.

"It's all a sham," Charlize shouted. "He tricked us into giving him costly gifts. His apartment upstairs—it's all packed away. He's running off with everything we gave him!"

But Maddox didn't run anywhere. He rolled onto his back, the crisp, white shirt crimson.

Charlize turned her face to look down at him, her chin sharp against the black shoulder of her dress. Her glare turned back to the stunned room. "Consider *that* when you decide what calls to make."

Silence. And then Charlize's gown rustled like ocean surf as she fled.

Gwen sprinted around the tables and dropped beside Maddox, ivory satin pooling around her. She laid her hand on his black lapel. When he didn't respond, she leaned her ear to his mouth. No breathing. She couldn't do CPR, not with all this blood, not with this kind of wound.

"Maddox, if you can hear me, thank you." She gripped his hand. "Thank you, and I'm so sorry."

This man didn't deserve to die alone. He didn't deserve to die, period.

She whipped her head toward the other guests.

Heather held a cell phone to her ear. Between the two women, a sea of shocked and frozen tenants stared not at her, but at Maddox, as they'd always done. Gwen searched their faces for one who cared. Some were doctors. Respected surgeons.

"Help!"

Like watching a cliff give way to erosion, one guest and then another and then most—all?—shifted their gaze from the bleeding man to the golden gifts he'd bestowed.

"Help!" The word tore from Gwen's lungs.

A pop. A piece of tape, popping free. Paper crinkled as a tenant loosened the wrapping. More guests followed suit, unwrapping the gifts.

She leaned farther over Maddox and prayed that he was already gone because if he wasn't, this would surely kill him. Crimson flowers of blood bloomed on her dress.

By the time the police arrived, only Gwen, Heather, and a hundred crumpled sheets of golden wrapping waited in the ballroom with Maddox's body.

When law enforcement allowed Gwen to leave, she returned to her apartment, her strappy heels as heavy as cinderblocks. Charlize and the others should've taken her to the bridge they hated so much, thrown her off, and watched her drown.

The police had arrested Charlize, but no punishment could undo to the horror of the crime.

Gwen would move. She couldn't stay here. It didn't matter what it cost to break the lease.

As far as she had seen, she and Heather were the only ones to leave the ballroom without opening their gifts, all Bibles. The fact that he'd included a card with her package this year had been intriguing before, but now, it shimmered as a lifeline. A note from Maddox. She slipped the card from under the ribbon of the gift.

Maddox had written in gold ink that shone in the light.

Gwendolyn:

Your neighbors have short-changed themselves year after year, refusing gifts in packages as beautiful as diamond necklaces and custom-made coats. They never suspected the additional value included with those gifts! Imagine how they would have treated gifts in puzzling, ugly, or sharp-edged packages.

I have waited for years for someone different.

But even you, Gwendolyn… Can you accept a gift you have no hope of earning, no matter how many hours you serve at the noblest of causes?

True gifts cannot be earned, but they can be refused in a myriad of ways. The gift in this box is no different.

Merry Christmas,

Maddox

She stared. The necklace and the coat were packages for something else? She slid her feet from the weights of her high heels and lifted the skirt of the stained gown to ease the way to the dresser where she kept the necklace's box. The velvet cushion dropped into her hand, and flat beneath it lay a one hundred dollar bill, folded around something else. Other one hundred dollar bills. Ten, in total. One thousand dollars.

She turned to the hook where the coat hung. With her seam ripper, she severed one thread along the bottom hem of the lining and then another until ten stitches had been broken, just enough to peek inside. More bills, all hundreds, formed a secondary lining under the silk, carefully tacked to the wool without leaving evidence on the coat's exterior. She'd have to remove all of the silk to see how much was there, but at the moment, the latest gift pressed more heavily. The gift he'd given his life to give.

She returned to this year's gold-wrapped box and opened the package to reveal a Bible. She flipped through the pages and discovered one highlighted verse.

For it is by grace you have been saved, through faith – and this not from yourselves, it is the gift of God.

She stared toward her window, her view of the bridge. After a moment, she flipped through the Bible again and found a single word – gave – highlighted in John 3:16.

Gwen slept little that night. When the sun touched the sky in the morning, she took the elevator to the top floor – Maddox's floor. As the doors opened, pounding echoed down the hall. She rounded the corner and stopped. Richard, at Maddox's closed door, clutched a Bible identical to hers. He backed up and raised a foot as if to kick in the door, but a man dressed in the building's grey uniform appeared from the stairwell. "Can I help you, sir?"

"Not unless you can unlock this."

The man pulled a key from his pocket, slid it into the lock, and swung the door wide. Richard stalked in. A silent moment passed before he marched back to the hall. "It's cleared out! Empty. Where's everything from last night? We gave him a *boat*! And he gives us this?" He shoved the Bible forward, and the man flinched. "This is ridiculous. A *boat*! He won't be using it now."

"Richard, correct?" The man took a white envelope from his pocket. "I was instructed to give you this. But to get it, you must return to me the Bible he gave you."

Richard narrowed his eyes, tilted his head, and slowly made the trade. He flipped open the envelope and looked inside. His shoulders dropped. "Fine."

The man turned to Gwen as Richard left.

"What was in the envelope?"

"Paperwork and keys to a boat, I believe. I'm sure there's something for you, too. He left a very long list." The man pulled a packet of papers from his back pocket and unfolded it.

"So he never intended to leave with all the gifts, like Charlize said?"

"Shall I check for your name?"

Gwen shook her head, clutching the Bible. "I won't trade this. I came…" Why had she come? To say goodbye? "Will there be a funeral?"

"I've heard no such plans. His family isn't local."

Three days later, a squeal echoed across the marble lobby as Gwen returned from apartment hunting.

"Paid?" Rachel stood in the doorway of the building manager's office. "Paid in full for life? When did he do this?"

Beginning with her feet, Gwen's entire body grew heavy. These days, in this building, the pronoun "he" rarely stood for anyone other than Maddox.

Grinning at whatever answer the building manager supplied, Rachel turned and hurried for the elevator. As she crossed nearby, Gwen raised a leaden hand. "What's going on?"

"Before he died, he paid our rent. The whole building. None of us have to pay rent as long as we live. Can you believe it?" She rolled her eyes and shook her head. "Unbelievable."

Gwen stared as Rachel floated away.

The apartment manager confirmed Rachel's story. "He loaded up some kind of fund with money, and the rent is paid out of the interest." The man took off his glasses and rubbed his eyes. "But you're 428, aren't you?"

"Yes. Why?"

"He didn't cover yours. The only one. I don't know what you did to him."

Gwen's face burned. In a stupor, she returned to her apartment, clutched a pen, and hunched over a sheet of loose leaf.

Maddox –

They despised you. They watched you die. I wish you had known that before you took care of them this way. Though I don't know why you kept me out of the arrangement, I appreciate being set apart from them. I want no share in their lives, and I would continue my plan to leave this place, regardless of rent payments.

I wish I could thank you for the gifts you've given me, specifically the reminder to accept my salvation as a gift. I have been a believer for years, yet still struggle in that area. Thank you.

This place is not the same without you. My comfort is that if you were a believer, you are in heaven, and there you must've had the merriest of Christmases.

Gwendolyn

Though the letter would be returned to her undeliverable and unopened, she mailed it to his old apartment in the name of closure.

A month later, a golden envelope slid out from among her bills. She turned it three times before tearing the seal to reveal a golden card, like the one Maddox gave with her last gift. The handwriting inside matched, down to the shiny golden ink.

Dear Gwendolyn:

The riches I've shared are not my own; they belong to my father. For a time, he has chosen to bless many, regardless of their response to him or to me. However, the day is coming when this will not be.

Life on this earth will never be free of troubles. However, in light of your letter, my father has granted that I may give you a new life. You will find a key and an address to your new home enclosed.

Though the season is past, allow me to end with this:

Merry Christmas. Maddox.

A key and a slip of paper rested in the crease at the bottom of the envelope.

London.

The address was in London. Gwen sank to a seat by the window that overlooked the bridge.

She'd seen his body taken away, covered with a sheet. She'd given the police a statement. She'd watched police tuck Charlize into the back of a squad car. Yet he'd written her back?

The money from the coat would cover the ticket.

What would happen when she arrived, what would be done with everything she left behind to go, she couldn't say, but she would go, and she wouldn't look back.

About the Author: Emily Conrad

Emily Conrad created her first stories in washable marker shortly after she learned to write. The marker gave way to a computer, and she is now a full-time writer and a member of American Christian Fiction Writers. She shares her 500 square-foot home with her husband and two rescue dogs.

Connect with her online at
www.emilyconraduthor.com or
www.facebook.com/emilyconradauthor.

Scripture quoted is NIV, Ephesians 2:8

Christmas Presence

by Kari Fischer

(Honorable Mention)

For the second time since he'd taken charge of Mia, Deputy
Nick Gardner had cause to panic. She should have been waiting
for him on the sidewalk in front of school. Yes, he was late, but
that didn't give her license to leave on her own. What could
happen to her in a small town? If the wrong people got a hold of
her, a lot.

He checked the playground. A couple of kids he recognized
played on the monkey bars. No Mia. He took the front stairs two
at a time to prowl the school's interior, starting with Mia's
classroom.

"Deputy Gardner." Like a praline left in the sun, Mrs.
Fielding's smile melted. She set aside her pen and gave him her
full attention. "Is there something wrong?"

His hand rested on his weapon as he surveyed the room,
confirming Mrs. Fielding was alone. "When did you last see Mia?"

Her brows knit. "She left with a woman about ten minutes
ago. I thought you knew."

"You let her leave with a stranger?"

"Mia wouldn't go with a person she doesn't know."

He nodded. Considering her late mother's history, full of spies and distrust, Mia had cause to be wary. And he had reason to be overprotective. "Can you describe this woman?"

"She was about five foot six, blonde hair to her shoulders, straight, not curly, and... and she looked like Mia's mother. At least, what I remember from a picture Mia showed me."

"Melanie's dead."

Mrs. Fielding's eyes moistened. "I remember. Mia told me how you protected her from her mother's enemies. Such a life for an eleven-year-old girl. Thank God she's here, where it's safe."

If she only knew... "Except, little girls can still run off without telling their guardians. I think I know where she might be. Thanks, Mrs. Fielding." Talking to Mia's teacher had given him time to organize a mental list of the girl's favorite places.

The bell jingled on the entrance to the Silver Feather Café, situated in downtown Sommers, two blocks from the sheriff's station. He zeroed in on a couple blondes in a booth at the window. Mia's hands twisted and turned in the air as she spoke, but with the din from other patrons, he couldn't hear what she said. From the back, the narrow shoulders and long hair could have belonged to Melanie. His heart skipped a beat, and a chill ran over his skin as if he'd seen a ghost.

Nick crossed the short distance and stopped at the table, hands on his duty belt, staring at Mia. She fell silent and looked at him. He fought the instinct to ream her for her disobedience. "Didn't I tell you to stay at school?"

"Yes, Daddy." She bowed her head.

He turned his attention to the woman sitting across from Mia. His jaw slackened. With her deep blue eyes, the graceful curves of her cheeks and chin, and her heart-shaped lips, she could have been Melanie's twin. If he hadn't seen his estranged wife's dead body for himself, he might have entertained the notion that he'd been given a second chance.

"So this is the legendary Commander Nick Gardner, Navy SEAL? The man who captured Mel's heart so many years ago." The woman smiled, a half smirk. "I'm Patrice Allen. Mel's sister."

Nick accepted Patrice's outstretched hand. His grip, often crushing, was more like a dead carp. "Melanie had a sister? She never mentioned any living relatives."

Patrice's smile widened, but her eyes were dull beneath her brows. "That sounds like my sister. Too much a spy. Personal information, like family details, kept on a need-to-know basis."

"We never had much time to dig deep into our personal lives." Memories of what he did know about his wife flooded his mind. "I'd like to see some identification, Ms. Allen."

"Mrs. Allen, actually." As she raised her right eyebrow, it disappeared beneath her cascading hair. Melanie had styled her hair to the left.

Patrice's appearance had to be a joke, someone's evil idea of reopening old wounds. Over a decade had passed, but the sight of this woman turned his insides out and reminded him of what he'd lost.

He tore his attention away from her and skimmed the information on Patrice's license. Afternoon light streamed through the café windows and illuminated the New York state holographic watermark. With a nod, he handed the identification back to her.

"Relative or not, Mia had no business leaving school grounds without informing me." His glance roved from Patrice to Mia, who slunk deeper into her seat.

"Now that things are settled with Melanie's estate—"

"It is? That's news to me. I wasn't even aware she had more than what she carried in her suitcases."

"That's no surprise." Patrice examined a manicured nail. She shook her head. "I'm sorry. I was never a fan of my sister's profession."

Nick leaned over the table edge. "Not many people in town know Melanie's business. We should take this someplace more private. No need for our personal affairs to be fodder for the rumor mill."

"I agree. Let's go."

Nick placed his hand on Mia's shoulder and led her from the café. Patrice dropped a few bills on the table and followed. All the way to the station, he mulled over the new information. If Melanie couldn't trust Nick to handle her affairs, why didn't she take Mia to Patrice the minute she knew their daughter was in danger? *She knew you could take care of her and keep her safe. And you did. I wish she'd told me she had family still alive.*

So many things between them had never been said. A gaping hole in his heart increased in size as he considered how much he'd missed.

"Where are we going?" Patrice's sneakers slapped the pavement, and she huffed a breath before catching up to Mia and Nick.

"The station." He reached for the door, pulled it open, and allowed the ladies to enter first.

The front office was empty, but Nick heard clinking in the direction of the break room. Someone was there, most likely someone he could trust. "Back at the café, you said something about Mel's estate?"

"I was Melanie's executor. She left everything in her accounts to Mia, and she indicated Mia should live with me and my husband." Patrice dug her hands into her back pockets.

"You can't be serious." Murmurs distracted him. Mia wasn't in the room. He recognized Deputy Chris Snow's voice, and he relaxed but remained on alert for whatever other bombs Patrice decided to unleash. "We should sit down and discuss this."

He lead her into his office.

"There's nothing to discuss, other than when you'll have Mia ready to leave." She took the chair he offered, her eyes sparkling like Melanie's when something excited her. "My husband and I don't have any children, and we've been on the adoption waiting list for years. I can assure you, Mia would be well taken care of in our home, and well loved."

"Whoa. What makes you think you can sweep in here and demand custody? I'm her father." He leaned his forearms on the desk. He stared across the surface like a man interrogating a prisoner.

Patrice mirrored his posture. "Your name isn't on the birth certificate."

Nick remained in his defensive position, unblinking. He wasn't about to go on Patrice's word. "I assume you have these papers with you?"

"In my purse."

She answered with too much confidence. Her eyes never blinked. Either she was being honest, or she believed her version of the truth. She pulled a few sheets of folded paper from her bag and shoved the stack at him. Birds twittered outside, and a car passed going too fast, judging by the engine noise. But Nick's attention riveted onto the Will that Melanie drew up not long before she died.

"I'd appreciate it if you could have her ready by Saturday. I have business back home. Not that I couldn't do it remotely, but I'd like to get Mia settled in before Christmas." Patrice grinned. "We're taking her to Colorado. I can't wait to teach her how to ski."

"You're not taking Mia anywhere until I can prove my claim." He pushed the papers at her. "Mel left her with me for safe keeping, and as her father, I take my job seriously. As a deputy, I have to look at all the facts before I determine anything."

"This Will is the final word."

"Don't be so sure, Mrs. Allen. I have my own arsenal, and you haven't given me a chance to produce it yet."

"I'll have my attorney on the line and clear this up in no time." Patrice strode to the door. She slammed the door on her way out.

"Mia. Let's go." Nick led Mia to his classic, cherry-red GTO convertible. His gaze swept the street, sidewalks, and parking lot for threats. He'd almost believed they could relax and live life, but Patrice's boasting was anything but benign. He needed help.

"Where are you going?" Patrice, who had been on the sidewalk with her cellphone pressed to her ear, followed Nick and Mia into the parking lot.

"Home. Go back to your motel and settle in."

Though the days had grown cooler, Nick put the top down for Mia. If Patrice Allen had her way, he might not have too many days left to savor his daughter's joy of riding with the wind in her hair, chattering about the day's events.

Patrice is right. I don't have anything to show the truth, but I know it in my soul. She's mine. How can anyone look at Mia and not see me in her face? I can't lose her, Lord. I love this girl more than anything. The woman is determined. So am I. Allow me to be victorious in this battle.

Mia stretched her hands to catch the air currents as he half listened to her talking. His mind, stuck on Patrice and her surprise attack, left him grinding in neutral. He glanced in the mirror. The gray SUV kept a safe distance behind his car, but she crept closer as he drove out of town. The woman was crazy if she thought he'd run.

"Daddy, can I get one for Christmas?"

"What? What do you want?"

Mia sighed. "I was hoping you'd say yes and not ask first. Then you'd have to do it."

He smiled in order to keep the sinking in his heart from transferring to his face. "I'm too smart for that, kiddo."

She settled into the seatback. "I want a puppy."

His brows rose over the rim of his sunglasses. "Oh, I don't know. Who's going to take it out when you're at school?"

"Uncle Skip. He's retired and home all the time, so Freddy could keep him company."

Nick put both hands on the steering wheel. "Freddy. You've already named him?"

"Uh huh. I even have a picture." The magazine photo of a yellow lab danced in the air, clamped between her fingertips. "This is what Freddy should look like."

Oh, brother.

Nick exhaled and ran a hand through his short-cropped hair. He had enough trouble with everyone crammed into the tiny three-bedroom cottage. He imagined a big, slobbery dog lumbering around the place, running into things with abandon. Their ship-shape home would turn into a scow.

As if she could read his mind, Mia said, "It's not like he wouldn't have space. When my room is done, I'll use my allowance and get a big, cushy doggie bed for him to sleep on."

"I'll think about it and talk to Skipper and Chris. They have to live with Freddy too, you know?"

"Yeah." She drew out the syllable, which Nick had learned meant she didn't expect her wish to come true.

Dear, God, when you brought Mia to me, in trouble, I never bargained for this. I have so much to learn. Teach me, and please, bring the truth to light. Mia might want a dog for Christmas, but I just want confirmation she's mine. Forever.

Tires crunched gravel as Nick pulled into the drive. Patrice parked behind him. He waited for her at the bottom porch step, while Mia raced inside the house. The screen door slammed behind her.

"Mia Diane, what have I told you about charging in like a herd of cattle?" Skipper's bellow filtered through the open window.

"Who's that?" Patrice's brow wrinkled. She gripped her purse strap.

"That's just Skipper. Captain Stuart Newman, my last commanding officer when we were in the SEALs. My other roommate, Chris Snow, was also a SEAL." He glared at her. "Why are you here?"

Patrice's eyebrow rose. "You have an unconventional household, Deputy. I'm curious what kind of people my niece has been entrusted to."

"Call me Nick. You'll find we're no different than anybody else." First names helped disarm people. He would use every trick he knew to win this war.

"Except you probably speak six languages and can incapacitate a man with a chicken bone."

She has Mel's sense of humor. "Skipper made fried chicken tonight."

She froze. He smiled and stepped aside to let her enter first. He would rather have encouraged her to leave, but too many questions needed answering. She presented an opportunity to unearth something he could use against her later.

"Where did Mia go?" Patrice turned in a slow arc in the living room. She scowled as if the lack of male trappings, like animal trophies or rugged furniture made from logs, disappointed her.

"Knowing her, she's in the bedroom, kicking off her shoes, pulling her homework from her backpack, and getting down to business." Nick smiled. Her routine had become a comfortable thread woven into the fabric of their unorthodox family.

Mia thumped down the hall to meet them in the living room. She clasped her books and a spiral notebook to her chest. "I always do my homework before supper. After we eat, I help Daddy or whoever is cleaning the kitchen, and then we play a game or two before bedtime."

"I wouldn't have imagined you as a board game kind of guy." Patrice crossed her arms. Her purse slipped off her shoulder, but she rescued it from dropping to the floor.

"We play a lot of Risk. Mia's sharp for her age."

"How old is she?"

"Almost twelve." Did she think she could trip him up with such an easy question?

"Who's your guest?" Skipper entered the room, dressed in khaki shorts and a bright yellow Hawaiian shirt. His graying hair had been buzzed close to his scalp to hide the fact he was balding. He wiped his hands on a towel. His gaze never left Patrice. "Brother, she looks like Melanie. Spit and image of her. Wow."

"I'm her sister, Patrice."

"A pleasure, ma'am." Skipper flashed a bright smile and buried her hand in his grip. "Care to stay for dinner? There's plenty." He glanced at Nick. "I have a feeling you two have some business that won't be finished with a short conversation."

"You nailed that one." Nick shifted his belt. On a normal evening, he would go to his room and change. Tonight, he'd stay in uniform and hope a constant reminder of his position would serve as a damper if the situation turned ugly. "Excuse me, I'm going to stow this." He unbuckled his belt as he slipped around Patrice.

"Mind if I tag along? I'd like to see how Mia's been living with you guys."

His first instinct was to disagree. But this would give him a chance to show off the work he and his friends had been doing on the house. Plus, he could provide proof that they maintained a comfortable home. "Be careful of the construction in the back. We're building a room for Mia."

"I see. What made you decide to do this?"

"When she and I came here, we thought our stay would be temporary." He pointed to his uniform. "But as you can see, circumstances changed. Skipper put together some drawings, and we've been working on the addition during every spare moment." He reached his bedroom. The door was missing, and studs cut off a third of the room. "This will be an extension of the hall leading to Mia's new room."

"Where does she sleep now? There?" Patrice jabbed an index finger at the cot beneath the west window.

"We're pressed for space, and since Mia's my daughter, I wouldn't ask my friends to bunk up together when it's their place.

We're still guests. Besides, the work is almost finished." He swept his hand toward the last room at the end of the hall. "We're shooting for Christmas. Between this and the shopping, Mia's going to have the best holiday ever."

"I was hoping she would." Patrice clasped her hands in front of her. She faced Nick and looked deep into his eyes. "It's almost Christmas. I'd rather not get the courts involved when it's obvious I have the law on my side."

"But I have blood on my side, and I'm not backing down until a lab proves it. You might as well get comfortable at the Sommers Inn, Mrs. Allen. My attorney will be getting a call from me tonight."

The slack-jawed, pale face staring at him was a picture he'd remember for a long time.

Nick flexed his arm one last time as dark red blood filled the tube. They could take a liter as far as he was concerned, as long as his DNA matched Mia's. The needle slithered from his vein. The phlebotomist affixed a bandage with a cotton ball trapped beneath, and he'd been dismissed. Mia's blood had been collected earlier.

His attorney, Shanna Reed, met him in the clinic's waiting room. "How do you feel?"

"It's three weeks until Christmas, and I have to spend my time proving what I already know in my heart. It's not right." He squeezed the bandage tighter over the puncture wound, a small sacrifice for the truth.

"Don't worry. Mrs. Allen's attorney has released copies of her documentation, but I'll petition the court to get the real pages. I have a team of forensics experts who can determine if Melanie wrote the instructions to her sister, or if they're a forgery." Shanna smiled. "Don't hold off on your holiday plans."

"Easier said than done. Patrice is sticking around. I'd hoped she'd go back to her job, but she can telecommute."

"I have someone looking into her and her husband. If the court sides with a *traditional* family, we have to be prepared to discredit the couple."

"No. Wait, Shanna, this is getting out of hand." Nick glanced around the empty waiting room. In the middle of the day, the doctor had no patients other than a crying child in one of the exam rooms. "I want Mia to be with me, but not at the expense of ruining someone's reputation."

"Don't worry. When the blood tests prove you're Mia's father, Patrice won't have anything to hold up her argument." She patted his arm. "Now, where's that faith of yours? Don't you think God will allow the truth to win?"

He narrowed his gaze. Was she mocking his beliefs or embracing them? He chose to accept her words as a pep talk. "I better get back to work."

"I'll keep in touch."

"I appreciate you flying here from DC to help me. I needed a friend on this case."

"Anything for you." She embraced him, then let him go the second her cell phone rang. "I'll keep in touch."

Nick returned to the station to wait out the afternoon. He picked up a creased copy of the weekly penny saver, rested his feet on the wooden desk's edge, and skimmed the ads. Someone had circled three lines in the middle of one page.

> *Yellow Lab Puppies in time for Christmas! Get some lovin' before they're all gone. To make this a holiday your child will never forget, call 555-7409 and ask for the Puppy Lady.*

The corner of Nick's mouth stretched into a smile. "Chris. You're ingenious."

"Thanks for noticing." Deputy Chris Snow appeared in the front office with a coffee cup in one hand. "It's been so slow around here, so I thought I'd snoop for you. You know, with your mind on this paternity thing, a puppy isn't on your radar." He gestured at the bandage with his cup. "How long before you know?"

"At least two weeks." Nick dropped his feet from the desk. He picked up a pencil and tapped the paper. "I'm gonna do it. I'm pulling the trigger on this one."

"What if, by some freak of injustice, you lose? Will Mrs. Allen be okay taking a dog too?"

"I don't care. This is the one thing in the world Mia wants, more than staying here." He tapped the pencil tip into the paper, creating graphite dots around the ad. "Worst thing that could happen is—no, I'm not going to think about it." He punched the number into his cell phone and listened to the ring.

"Thank you for calling the Puppy Lady Kennel and Grooming Parlor, this is the Puppy Lady speaking. How may I help you?"

Nick's smile stretched into a grin. "I want to make this the best Christmas my daughter has ever had. Owning a yellow lab puppy would do it." *And knowing for sure we're family.*

As Nick ended the call, Patrice's SUV pulled up to the station. She got out of the passenger side. She entered the station with a man who looked older, with a lot of living trapped in the crinkles at the corners of his eyes and around his mouth. His styled hair was graying. But his slim form moved with a posture that would make a drill instructor proud. Old, but not ready for the rocking chair yet.

"Nick, Chris, this is my husband Daniel. Dan, these are the guys I was telling you about. Skipper is at home."

"Your husband. He's here because… why?" Nick scratched his eyebrow. He hadn't meant for his question to come out so defensive, but it was too late now to take it back.

Dan put an arm around Patrice's shoulders. "We were hoping to get this over with before Christmas, so we can take Mia to

Disney World for the holiday. Then we'll go back home after the new year."

"Disney World." Chris grunted. He swigged his coffee and retreated to the break room.

Dan raised an eyebrow.

Nick pulled on his duty belt as he stood. "We've taken Mia a couple times already. She thought it was okay."

Dan pressed his lips together, squinted, and looked at Patrice. "We'll think of something, honey."

"Wait a second. I thought you were taking her to Colorado." Nick stared at Patrice.

She shrugged. "Change of plans."

"Nice to know you're flexible. Speaking of, did you turn over the documents to my attorney?" He held up his phone. "If not, I can have her come over and pick them up. She's in town."

"Not necessary. We met her at the motel. If she destroys anything—"

"Funny, I was worried about you manufacturing evidence."

Patrice's gaze aimed at the weekly paper Nick left on the desk. He waited for her to say something.

Dan crashed through the ice building in the air. "If you don't mind, we'd like to take Mia to dinner tonight. I haven't met her yet, and I'd like to help make this transition go as smooth as possible."

"Why don't you come to our house for dinner?" Chris blurted his suggestion as he returned to the main office from the break room.

God bless you. Until the court decided Mia's custody, Nick wouldn't leave her alone with the couple. He'd seen too many FBI bulletins regarding children stolen by people fighting over custody. "That's a great idea, Chris. Skipper always makes enough for guests. It's a southern thing."

"All right. We'll be there."

There were only so many dinners with the Allens that Nick could take. After two weeks, his plan to glean information had backfired. They were nice people, and Mia grew to like them. This wasn't supposed to happen.

Every day, the mailbox sang its high-pitched, rheumatic groan as he shut the door with the heel of his hand. He rifled through the envelopes. Bills, magazines or catalogs, but nothing with a state seal. A short horn burst behind him. Nick dodged out of the way, and Chris steered his cruiser into the driveway. Nick wandered to the porch. Chris caught up with him.

"Nothing yet?"

"The results should have been here by now. I'm hoping maybe Shanna received them."

Chris stared at his boots, then raised his head. "I'm sorry. This waiting is about to drive Skipper and me nuts. I can't imagine how you do it."

"I don't know how much longer I can." He released a pent-up breath and dropped his shoulders. "One week until Christmas, and I don't think the Allens are going to wait much longer. Patrice asked if she and Dan could take Mia to the Black Cow tonight."

"That's her favorite place to eat. What did you say?"

Nick released a shuddering breath. "Did I do the right thing by saying yes? I think we're to the point where I expect they won't run off with her. But then, I second guess myself."

"You have to trust them sometime. Face it, they're family. This has to end on amicable terms, or Mia might get hurt."

"I shouldn't have let them get close."

"You did the right and honorable thing. Don't ever regret it."

"I'd do anything for Mia."

"So would we. Come on inside. Smells like Skipper's made his fried chicken. Too bad Mia's going to miss it."

Until Chris mentioned Mia, his stomach rumbled in anticipation. The empty space at the kitchen table inflamed his sense of loneliness. He closed his eyes until the pain from imagining Mia gone forever rolled over him and left his soul bleeding.

"You're just pushing your food around." Beneath the overhead lamp, Skipper's pale eyes deepened to sea green. He frowned as he stared at Nick. His fork dangled over his almost empty plate. "We're also in this battle, and the good Lord will put Mia in the home where she belongs. In my opinion, that's ours." He leveled his fork at Nick. "But whatever happens, it's His will. Don't forget."

"Of course, Skipper." Nick pushed his chair away from the table. "I'm going to my room to pray."

As he exited the kitchen, footsteps thumped on the porch. Maybe Dan and Patrice brought Mia home early. Or she got sick. He squelched the scenarios running through his brain and hurried to the door. Under the porch light, Deputy Perry stood with hands on his belt. Deep shadows turned his face into a map of anxiety.

"Nick, I just received a report of an accident on the highway near the Black Cow. The description of the vehicle was a gray SUV, three passengers."

"Mia." Nick burst from the house and ran to the cruiser waiting at the end of the drive. Perry caught up, backed out of the driveway, and sped to the scene with flashers running.

"Maybe it's someone else's vehicle." Nick tried to talk himself out of his fears.

Perry didn't respond. He gripped the steering wheel and pressed the accelerator to the floor when they hit the village limits. Within minutes, they arrived on the fringe of red and blue lights piercing the darkness. Bright halogen lights illuminated the mangled hulks of two vehicles, the gray SUV and a red sedan, in the left turn lane which led to the Black Cow's driveway. Dozens of people stood outside their cars in the parking lot and gawked, while eating and drinking, as if what they saw had happened on a movie screen.

Nick searched the panorama for Mia. Patrice sat on an ambulance bumper with a large gauze pad against her bare upper arm. Her ripped sleeve drooped, soaked with blood. His stomach lurched.

"Patrice. What happened?" He bent to her level, out of the way for the paramedic to do his job.

"Dan was turning in to the restaurant, and this guy tore out of the drive over there." She pointed into the darkness. Moving her injured arm cost her, and she winced. "He plowed into our side."

"But Mia's okay, right?" Nick glanced at the SUV's crumpled passenger doors.

Firefighters wedged a prying tool into the gap between the body and the door. A gurney stood by. Movement inside gave him hope, until he realized it was a paramedic and not Mia.

"Why don't they get her from the driver's side? Where's your husband? Patrice?"

"He's in this ambulance. They're taking us to the hospital soon for evaluation." She looked at him. "We were laughing and having a good time. Then one second later - bam."

"Are you saying Dan wasn't paying attention? How could he be so irresponsible? If something happens to Mia..." He clamped his hands behind his head, his mind full of threats he was better off not spewing.

"Don't tell me you've never done anything like take your eyes off the road for a second or two."

A heavy chill trickled from Nick's head to his toes. "One second is all it takes. I trusted you with my daughter, and look what happened."

"It was an accident. Unless you've turned into God, I'd like to see you try to stop random incidents from happening."

Perry pulled Nick away from Patrice. "Come on, man. I know how you feel, but cut her a break. It's not like they harmed Mia on purpose."

Nick shrugged off Perry's grip. "My daughter's life is at stake, in more ways than one. She belongs with me. I can keep her safe."

He strode across the highway, stepped over a piece of what might have been the sedan's bumper, and approached the SUV. Two small bare feet appeared, followed by the rest of Mia's still, pale form. Two firefighters carried her on a back board to the gurney. A third man held aloft an IV bag. Nick snatched it from his hand.

"I'm her father. I'm going with her to the hospital."

"Sure thing, Deputy."

Nick hadn't changed out of his uniform after work, which came in handy on the scene. He lost sight of Patrice, but he didn't care. If he had his way, the couple would never see Mia again. But at the moment, the figure of his injured little girl took his world and shook it to the foundation.

The dry-erase board across from Mia's bed announced the date, December 26, beside a smiling snowman. Mia wore a frown as unlike the cartoon character as she could get. "Christmas is over, Daddy. I was supposed to sing in church, and dance with the angels. It was going to be really cool."

"I'm glad you're not dancing with the real angels, at least, not yet." His cell phone rang. He glanced at the screen and read the text from Chris.

The mission is a go.

"We'll celebrate even if Christmas is over, and be glad you're going to be okay. Nothing else matters to me." Nick squeezed her hand.

"But if Aunt Patrice and Uncle Dan take me away, I won't get to be with you." Her brown eyes, much like his, glistened.

His throat closed up. He couldn't find the words to comfort her, because without the DNA test, he had no legal basis to keep Mia in his home.

Tinny jingling echoed in the hall. Children shouted and squealed in delight. "Santa! Santa!"

"Hey, did you hear that? Santa must be a little behind on his deliveries." Nick smiled. "Or his GPS was off and he missed our house on Christmas Eve."

Mia rolled her eyes. "You know there's no Santa Claus, right?"

"No Santa? Then who's that?" He pointed to the doorway, where a man dressed in an overstuffed red coat and pants trimmed in white fur lumbered into the room.

His beard slipped a little when he worked up a hearty ho-ho.

"Nice try, Uncle Skip. I know it's you." Mia's eyes sparkled, and she giggled.

Skipper's arms dropped to his sides, his shoulders sagged, and he set a large bag on the floor. "You mean I braved all those kids mauling me for nothing?"

Mia grinned. "It was sweet."

"We wanted to make it a special day for you, hon." Skipper pulled off the beard as he approached the bed. He kissed her forehead. "How are you feeling?"

"Great, except for missing all the fun." She pouted.

"That's why I'm here."

"Where's Uncle Chris?" Mia leaned to the side, searching for him.

"He'll be here in a minute. We ran into Shanna at the elevator."

At that moment, Chris and Shanna entered the room. They smiled at one another as if they were involved in a conspiracy. Nick stared at Chris, who smiled wider and hid a gift-wrapped box behind his back. Puppy-sized, if Nick wasn't mistaken.

"I don't want to take up your celebration time, so I'll get right to business." Shanna reached into her purse and extracted an envelope. "I received this after hounding the lab. There was a mix-up in the department responsible for sending these notices. They had your address wrong. You should have received this earlier in the week."

"Do you know what it says?"

"The seal hasn't been broken yet."

Nick ripped the short side of the envelope with care. Chris and Skipper leaned closer, along with Shanna. Mia sat straighter, hands clasped tight. He grasped the paper inside, unfolded the sheet, and stared at the short but succinct letter.

His hands shook, rattling the papers as he scanned the letter and reread it, thinking he'd misinterpreted the message.

"Daddy. What is it? What's wrong?"

He couldn't see more than a blob of blonde hair, blue eyes, and four and a half feet of anxiety sitting in bed.

"I just got the best Christmas present ever, sweetie. Come on and give your Daddy a hug." The paper crinkled and fell to the floor. He gathered Mia in his arms.

"Praise God." Skipper whispered his thanks.

"Amen." Chris added his agreement.

"Congratulations, Nick, and Mia. But my work isn't done." At the door, she turned. "Merry Christmas to all of you."

"It is now." Nick kissed the top of Mia's head. He held her a long time, unconcerned about the growing dampness on his shirt soaking in his daughter's happy tears.

Woof! Woof, woof!

"Uh-oh. We better let Mia open this now." Chris set the box on the bed.

Mia scooted closer to the box and tugged at the wide ribbon holding the box together. The satin fell away, and she threw off the cover. Her mouth formed a large 'o'.

"Freddy! You brought Freddy here," Mia cried and wrapped her arms around the yellow lab puppy Chris lifted and set on the mattress.

Skipper held a finger to his lips. "Shh. We can't alert the staff."

Through a curtain of moisture, Nick watched Mia snuggle the puppy. "How did you keep him quiet all the way through the hospital?"

Chris shrugged. "Let's call it a Christmas miracle."

Mia kissed the top of Freddy's head, then slipped an arm around Nick. "This is the best Christmas ever. We both have a family forever. Thank you, Daddy."

Nick held her tight. *No. Thank God for making your presence the best present.*

About the Author: Kari Fischer

 By day, Kari is a secretary at a large corporation. By night and on weekends, curled up with her iPad, she's creating another story. Several instructors told her she had a gift for writing, but she never took them seriously. In 1996, she began dabbling in the world of fan fiction, influenced by television shows such as "Due South" and "Burn Notice." She had written nearly 300 pieces of fan fiction before self-publishing the novella "Wolves and Sheep Don't Mix" in 2012. She self-published "Bonded By Blood" in 2014. The short story you just read is based on "Bonded By Blood."

Kari lives in Wisconsin with her husband and two cats, Callie and Mr. Finley. When she's not writing, or volunteering with the Sheboygan County United Way Lunch Buddy program, she and her husband spend time at the range or hit the road looking for new places to visit.

Email: karifischer@charter.net
Website: www.karifischer.net
Twitter: https://twitter.com/WritePassion
Facebook: https://www.facebook.com/WritePassion

Just Another Navidad

by Allison K. Garcia
(Honorable Mention)

The smell of chicken tamales with green salsa steaming in cornhusks inside a pot nearly as tall as him, sitting on top of a small, gas stove. The sound of *Abuela* humming along with the Christmas songs on the radio while she prepared the *champurrado* to drink from warm ceramic mugs after they came back from *Misa de Gallo*, the midnight mass at Santa Cecilia, their neighborhood's chapel. The feel of the *peso* between his fingers as he tap-tap-tapped it on the metal door of their neighbors' cement houses, the other children and he playing Mary and Joseph looking for a place to lay their heads during *Las Posadas*. The taste of the honey, cinnamon, and brown sugar when he bit into a *buñuelo*, its crunchy crust sticking on his lips. The flashes and pops of colorful fireworks as the block celebrated the arrival of baby Jesus.

Christmas in his childhood home of Guadalajara, Mexico.

Alberto glanced around him. Where were those smells, those colors, those sounds now? Their chilly, drab trailer showed no signs of the approaching holiday, other than a roughly drawn Santa Claus stuck to the fridge with a magnetized bottle-opener. The American Christmases he had grown up seeing in the movies were bright, happy occasions, filled with roast turkeys and colorful Christmas lights and cold-nosed children singing house-to-house as soft, moonlit snow fell quietly around them.

His cold-nosed children didn't sing Christmas songs as they stared at the glowing television screen; they couldn't afford the dollar-store strands of outdoor lights, let alone the additional charges on their astronomical electric bill for their poorly insulated trailer; and the only turkeys he saw were the hundreds per day he gutted at the processing plant. The one thing Hollywood seemed to get right was the freezing cold temperature.

Compared to the moderate climate of Guadalajara, Virginia's wintery weather was a shock to the system. His wife, Rosa, still wasn't used to it, five years after they moved here with their son, Daniel, then a wiggly three-year-old, and their daughter, Yesica, still in the womb. Rosa began cranking up the heat in September and didn't switch back to short sleeve shirts until May.

But Alberto liked the cold. Not all the time, especially not the frigid days that bit into your bones. He preferred the days that turned just the right temperature for a light, fluffy snow that dusted the Blue Ridge Mountains with a white blanket for the winter, where the sunrise and sunset would make the dry cornfields look like a shimmering, icy rainbow.

Some days the view was the only thing that lifted his spirits on his long, slow commute on his scooter to and from work through the winding, country roads that led from the trailer park into the next town over. Even after his friend "fixed" the bike by taking out the piece that wouldn't allow it to go over thirty miles per hour, it only hit fifty on a warm day along a long stretch of flat, straight road. Usually, the fifteen-mile journey took about forty minutes with all the curves and annoyed drivers honking to pass him.

"*Un día te van a chocar,*" Rosa would tell him, a worried look on her face. *One day you're going to crash.*

She was probably right. With the combination of weather this year and the hurried drivers, it was getting pretty dangerous. But he had no other option. They couldn't afford to buy a car and to pay for it to be plated and insured. For now, the aging scooter would have to do.

It had served him well for three years already, what was one more winter?

He sighed and finished his cup of coffee and the last mouthful of quesadilla drizzled in hot sauce. Pulling on several layers of clothing and his bright yellow work boots before topping it off with his backpack, filled with his lunch and work uniform, he headed out for another double shift.

He grunted. Drizzle. The cold rain stung his face like tiny daggers as his bike gained speed onto the back road. At this moment, the Christmases of his childhood seemed farther away than ever.

Fourteen hours later, Alberto turned into their muddy driveway. Stiff and chilled to the bone, he pried himself off his scooter and attempted to avoid the half-frozen puddles on his way to the rickety wooden steps under the front door. With a smile, he inhaled the aroma that greeted him at the door.

"¡*Qué rico!*" *Delicious.* He oohed as he stepped inside.

"Don't get excited. We're not allowed to eat any." Daniel looked over long enough from the television to give his father a frown.

Alberto raised an eyebrow. "*¿Y por qué no?*" *Why not?* After peeling off the layers of soggy clothes and plopping them on top of the washing machine, he came up behind his aproned wife and wrapped her in a hug.

"*Los vamos a vender,*" Yesica squeaked in an excited voice as she stirred the large bowl of *masa* that sat on the floor. *We're going to sell them.* She had one leg on either side to keep the bowl from spinning as both of her small, floured hands gripped the large wooden spoon like it could fly away at any moment.

Rosa only sold *tamales* when things got tight. Even with the overtime, they were struggling this year. After tax time things always loosened up a little, but usually the winter months brought extra costs and by Christmas, they were broke. She pointed her lips towards the electric bill on the counter and let out a long, quiet sigh.

He wanted to tell her things would be okay, but the words caught in his throat. Instead, he pushed her long, black hair out of the way with his nose and kissed her gently on the neck, holding her tighter and swaying her back and forth. He cleared his throat and bent down to kiss Yesica on the top of her head, picking out a couple chunks of dried corn dough from her hair. She wore a small, pink apron over her princess pajamas, which were faded a soft pink by the dusting of corn flour covering nearly every inch of her. He smiled and stood back up, ignoring the dull ache in his back.

Girls in bikinis danced in a music video on the television screen. A man covered in thick gold jewelry rapped a tune and gestured inappropriately towards the women. Alberto frowned, watching as Daniel bobbed his head to the beat and stuck his orange-stained fingers back into a bag of junk food. He looked back and forth from his son, one leg up on the arm of the couch and the other dangling a couple inches from the floor, and to his wife and daughter, covered with food and sweat, working to support the household.

He crossed his arms and raised his voice over the loud music. *"Oye, Daniel. Ven aquí. Ayúdale a tu mamá con los tamales."* Daniel, *come here and help your mother with the tamales.*

"Ew." He scrunched up his nose. "That's girls' work."

"Oh, ¿*sí*?" Alberto rolled up his sleeves and washed his hands and arms in the sink. He grabbed an apron from a hook on the wall near the fridge, stuck it over his head, and wrapped the strings around his slim waist then tied it in the front. Pushing his thick hair from his face, he stood next to Rosa. *"¿Te hecho una mano?"* Would you like a hand?

Rosa's dark brown eyes crinkled into a smile. She rubbed the small of his back and nodded. *"Sí. Gracias, amor."* Yes, thank you, honey.

Alberto glanced at Daniel out of his periphery as he shredded the chicken with his tired fingers. He had already seen more poultry today than any man should see in a lifetime, but he pushed past the pain of carpel tunnel that throbbed and pulsed throughout his joints. It was worth it. Daniel had stopped looking at the video and was looking into the kitchen.

Humming "Jingle Bells," Alberto tossed the chicken into a large bowl as Rosa took over working on the *masa* and gave Yesica the task of sweeping up the floor.

"Jinga Bews, Jinga Bews, Jinga aaaah da way," Yesica sang while she pushed the corn dough dusting the floor into small piles with her child-sized, pink broom.

Daniel stood up and wandered over to the kitchen. *"¿Te ayudo, Mami?"* Can I help you, Mommy?

"¿No que era trabajo de niñas?" Rosa asked with twitch of a smile. *I thought that was girls' work?*

Daniel shrugged, not making eye contact. "All the good chefs on TV are men."

"Oh, *¿sí?*" Alberto asked, poking him in the ribs.

His son giggled and wriggled away. "Stop, stop," he cried, his laughter crescendoing.

"Cosquillitas," Yesica shrieked and attacked Alberto with her tiny fingers. *Tickles.*

Soon the kitchen was filled with cries of laughter.

"Okay, okay, *ya ya ya,*" Rosa gasped, calling an end to the silliness. She wiped tears from her eyes with the inside of her shirt collar.

Working together, they spread the *masa* onto the softened husks and put a few pieces of chicken in green salsa in the center. They wrapped them up and placed them in the large *tamalera*. The two hundred tamales sold at two dollars each would almost be enough to pay that month's light bill.

Daniel helped Alberto lift the heavy pot onto the stove, and Rosa poured water into the bottom through an empty space between the packed tamales. She turned on the burners at the same moment someone knocked on their door.

"¿Quién será?" Alberto raised an eyebrow. Who could that be?

Rosa frowned and shrugged. "No sé." I don't know.

"I'll get it," Daniel announced, tossing his apron on the back of a kitchen chair.

The faint sound of singing outside the trailer led Alberto and his wife to exchange glances and follow Daniel towards the door. As it opened, they all stood in silence, mouths agape.

A group of about twenty men, women, and children, bundled up in thick coats, hats, and scarves had gathered on and around their porch steps and were singing "Campanas de Belén," one of Alberto's favorite Mexican Christmas carols. Yesica encircled her arms around Rosa's leg and peeked out from behind her apron at the singers.

Alberto draped his arm over Daniel's shoulders and reached out to hold Rosa's hand. A familiar joy filled his heart so warmly that he barely felt the freezing air around him. He looked at the smiling faces of the carolers, a mix of Americans and Latinos. A few faces he recognized from the trailer park. The rest were strangers.

A young, blonde woman waved at Daniel.

"Ah." Daniel looked up at his father. "I know her. She works at the afterschool program."

"De la iglesia," Alberto whispered to Rosa, pointing his head towards the church down the hill at the bottom of the trailer park. From the church.

Rosa nodded, her face more serene than he had seen in years.

After a bilingual version of "Silent Night" and a final song of "Feliz Navidad," his family burst into applause.

"*Gracias,*" Rosa exclaimed. She and Alberto shook the hands of the carolers closest to the front.

Several of them came over and high-fived or hugged Daniel before continuing on to the next trailer.

A middle-aged man with peppered black hair stepped forward. "*Somos de la iglesia Dove Peak.*" *We're from Dove Peak Church.* He handed them a flier, one side in English and the other in Spanish. "*Soy el pastor. Me llamo Raimundo.*" *I'm the pastor. My name is Raimundo.* He nodded to the thin blonde on his right. "*Y mi esposa, Patty.*" *And my wife, Patty.*

His wife was an American with a huge smile and bright blue eyes. She leaned over towards Daniel and ruffled his hair. "*Ya conozco a Daniel y Rosa.*" *I already know Daniel and Rosa.* She turned to Alberto's wife and shook her hand with a brief kiss on the cheek. "*¿Cómo estás?*" *How are you?* She gently lifted the apron and said in a higher-pitched voice. "*Yesiquita ¿cómo estás?*" *Little Yesica, how are you?*

Yesica giggled and hid her face again against Rosa's leg.

Pastor Raimundo pointed to the flier, an invitation to the Christmas Eve service next week, explaining the party afterwards where there would be food and games.

"*Muchas gracias.*" *Thank you so much.* Alberto smiled. They waited until everyone had gotten out of their driveway and then closed the door.

"*Ay, qué bonito,*" Rosa exclaimed with a satisfied sigh. *How nice.*

Daniel nodded. "Miss Patty is really nice. *Es mi favorita.*" *She is my favorite.*

Alberto had never before met anyone from the church down the hill. He was always working when the volunteers brought Daniel home from the afterschool program and when they had their special events, which never fit into their busy schedule. He tacked the flier onto the fridge next to Santa and returned to the tamales.

A pair of bright lights. The screech of car tires. Breaking glass. Blood. The blinking lights of an ambulance. Murmurs in English around him.

Beeps and clicks sounded around him but Alberto's eyelids were too heavy to open. Rosa's voice and then darkness.

More beeps and clicks. This time he was able to see through his squinted eyes. The fluorescent lights were bright above him. He tried to speak but his throat was raw and something was in his mouth. The room spun and turned to black again.

A pale arm reached over him. He moaned.

"Mr. Gonzalez?" A woman hovered. "I'm just fixing your IV."

"*¿Qué pasó?*" he croaked. "*¿Dónde estoy?*" *What happened? Where am I?*

"In the hospital. You had an accident." She shined a bright light in his left eye and then his right. "*Accidente,*" she spoke with a thick Southern drawl.

Blinking, he looked around the blurry room. Everything was a pale shade of green, including the cushions on the rocking chair next to his bed. A blue coat lay on the back of the chair. Rosa's coat. "Rosa?"

"She's in the cafeteria," the nurse said with a smile. "She'll be back soon. *Mucho pronto.*"

"*¿Y mis niños?*"

"Hmm?" The nurse checked the levels on a machine.

"My childrens."

"They were here earlier. I think a neighbor's taking care of them."

Alberto adjusted himself in the bed and searing pain shot through his left side. Glancing down, he saw his left arm was in a cast all the way up to his shoulder. He couldn't move it and when he tried, he cried out.

"Don't try to move, Mr. Gonzalez. I'm gonna give you this for the pain. *Medicina,*" she added louder. "Try to get some sleep."

The IV entrance on his right arm got warm and the room faded away again.

When Alberto awoke, a familiar-looking blonde sat at his right side with Rosa, chatting in Spanish, as a woman in blue scrubs examined a chart in her slender fingers. Alberto blinked a few times and swallowed, his throat scratchy.

"Good morning, Mr. Gonzalez." The middle-aged doctor with bright red glasses and short, brunette hair leaned closer to him.

"*Buenos días, Señor Gonzalez,*" the blonde woman echoed.

He was able to wheeze out a raspy reply.

"I'm Dr. Kelton, and this is your interpreter. She's going to help me explain what happened."

The interpreter introduced herself as Patty, and a vague image of her singing Christmas carols flashed into his mind. The pastor's wife. He glanced down at her dark purple shirt where she wore an official hospital badge.

Rosa, tearful, lightly squeezed his right hand and gave him a weak smile.

As he returned his focus back to the doctor, his eyes struggled to follow as fast as usual, like they were swimming through a hazy liquid. The lights on the ceiling and walls had a fuzzy halo around them.

"You're going to feel groggy for the next day or two," the doctor explained with Patty interpreting her words in quick repetition. "We've got you on some heavy pain medications. You had a very serious accident. The EMT on the scene spoke with the other driver involved in the accident who said his car slid out of control on a patch of black ice and side-swiped your scooter, knocking you down an embankment. You're lucky to be alive."

Rosa choked back a sob.

Alberto's heart pounded. The beeping sped up on the monitor next to him. He ran his thumb over the back of Rosa's hand.

"We were able to save your left arm. It was in pretty bad shape." She pointed to a spot a few inches above his wrist. "The bone here was protruding from your forearm. Thankfully, it didn't break higher up your arm and puncture an artery. You underwent two surgeries, and we had to do a skin graft, so you might find that your buttocks are a little sore and itchy for a while."

The words swirled around him like fruit in a blender, mixed in with images of exorbitant hospital bills, feelings of fear and sadness, and pictures of Rosa, Daniel, and Yesica. He fought back tears and let out a slow, cooling breath. "When I can go back to work, *Doctora*?"

She grimaced and shook her head. "Not for a while. You also broke a few ribs, which will make it hard to get around for several weeks. You'll need weeks of physical therapy once the cast is off to regain control of the functions of your hand and arm. It really depends on how the therapy goes and what type of job you have."

"I work for the poultry plant."

Dr. Kelton looked down at the chart and swallowed. "I'm afraid you may not be able to do that sort of work anymore. With the amount of injury you have sustained, it would take a miracle to get your fine motor skills in that hand back to that level."

The wind gushed out of him like a sucker punch to the gut, and he was unable to reply. He stared at his left arm, laying innocently in the large, blue cast, hiding a horrific truth underneath its smooth surface.

The doctor put her hand on his lower leg over the itchy, white sheet. "I know this is a lot to absorb. I'll give you and your wife some time to talk about what this might mean for your family."

Alberto lay in silence until a nurse from earlier knocked and brought a large cup of ice water. The interpreter cleared her throat.

Rosa jumped and let go of the woman's hand. "*Ay, perdón,*" *Oh, sorry,* she apologized, her cheeks darkening a shade pinker.

Patty smiled and patted Rosa's arm. "*Está bien. Mi esposo le está visitando otro paciente. ¿Le gustaría que venga para orar con ustedes?*" *It's fine. My husband is visiting another patient. Would you like him to come pray with you?*

What difference would a visit from the pastor make? A couple prayers wouldn't change the fact that their family was in serious trouble. Yet something inside him tugged. He glanced over to Rosa, whose eyes were brimming with tears. A look of anticipation floated in her eyes. He shrugged and gave a slight nod. "Okay, *gracias.*"

After Patty left, he and Rosa didn't speak. The worry seemed to consume the very air around them, like a fire. The television whispered on the wall and the steady hum of machines droned on to his left. The second hand on the clock grew louder as the minutes passed. Outside the window, he had a view of the roof of the floor below them, the parking lot, and, in the distance, snow-capped mountains. The sky was a dull gray.

Alberto sipped his ice water and ignored the throbbing pain pulsing up and down his arm.

Someone knocked on the door.

"*Entre,*" Alberto called, and Pastor Raimundo stepped into the cool room.

"*Buenos días.*" Raimundo shook their hands, a concerned look on his face. "*¿Qué pasó?*" *What happened?*

Alberto explained about the accident.

"Wow, *qué horrible.*" *How horrible.* Raimundo clicked his tongue then let out a puff of air, shaking his head. "*¿Puedo orar por ustedes?*" *Can I pray for you?* He held out a hand to each of them.

Alberto shrugged and Rosa nodded.

Raimundo clasped Rosa's right hand and put his other on Alberto's cast. They closed their eyes as he prayed in a soft, friendly tone, thanking God for protecting Alberto during the accident, for his survival, and asking for full healing and understanding.

Some of the heaviness resting in Alberto's chest lifted as he echoed an *"Amén."*

"Gracias." Rosa's voice cracked.

Pastor Raimundo nodded his head. *"De nada."* You're welcome. He chatted with them until the nurse came to give Alberto his next dose of pain medication.

Alberto leaned back as the pulsating pain dulled in intensity.

Rosa sighed and squeezed his hand, her cheeks raised into a soft smile.

A lump settled in his throat. That smile was well worth the visit.

Three days later, the morning before Christmas Eve, Pastor Raimundo and his wife picked up Alberto in their brown, beat-up station wagon at the hospital entrance to drive him back to his trailer. Alberto told them he could get a taxi back for only a few dollars, but they insisted.

New roads made the journey quick. Only a handful of minutes later, they pulled up to the driveway, empty now without his totaled scooter. A rush of emotions surged from his stomach into his heart like a tidal wave. He pushed them down and forced a smile as Yesica jumped up and down on the front steps, waving wildly.

"Papá, Papá," she cried out.

Daniel stood next to her, looking with a furrowed brow at the large cast on his father's arm. Rosa stood behind them, a hand on the shoulder of each child.

Alberto opened the car door, and Yesica nearly tackled him before he could tell her to be careful. He turned his torso in time to prevent her from colliding with his arm. Instead, she wrapped her thin arms around his waist and gave him a squeeze, her head pressed into his stomach and pushing on his sore ribs.

"Okay, okay." Rosa peeled her off, one arm at a time, picked her up, and plopped her onto her aproned hip. "*Te amo.*" *I love you*, his wife whispered in his ear as she kissed him on the cheek. She smelled like tamales and the inexpensive, floral perfume he got her for her birthday last year.

"*Te amo,*" he whispered back, then turned his focus to Daniel, who stood nearby, worry clouding his face. Alberto nodded him over and pulled him in for a hug. "*Todo va a estar bien.*" *Everything is going to be okay.* He tried to sound confident.

But he was no longer sure of anything. If he couldn't get another job soon, they would have to sell the trailer and go back to Mexico to live with his mother. Virginia was safer and had better schools and opportunities for the children, but both of their families were still in Mexico and no one here could support them. There would be no other option.

"*Espero que puedan venir al servicio de Nochebuena.*" *I hope that you can come to the Christmas Eve service.* Raimundo gave Alberto a pat on the back.

With all the craziness surrounding the accident, Alberto had forgotten all about the Christmas Eve service. "*Si Dios quiere.*" *Yes, God willing.* He answered automatically and mustered a tired smile. He hadn't planned on going and, given all that was happening, he was even less interested than when the invitation was first presented. There was a part of him that regretted the internal decision he had already made, whether it was guilt or curiosity. But it would take more than that to drag him out of the house. All he wanted to do was rest and spend time with his family. Forget the *Navidades* from his youth; he was happy to have it be just another day.

The pastor nodded, seeming to get the message hidden behind his weak response. *"Claro."* *Of course.* Giving him another pat on the back, he stepped over to his wife, who was chatting up a storm with Rosa and the kids.

Alberto caught a passing remark, something about animals and angels.

"Bueno, vámonos, amor." *Good, let's go, honey,* Raimundo said in a gentle though insistent tone, putting his arm around Patty's shoulder and nodding towards the car.

She said her goodbyes, leaving the Gonzalez family to continue with their reunion.

"Mira, Papá." *Look, Daddy!* Yesica opened the front door, hopping from foot to foot.

The inside of the trailer was decorated with chains of red, white, and green paper links draped from the corners to the middle of the room. White napkin snowflakes dropped down from the ceiling with twist ties and tape. A cheap, plastic tree, about the height of Yesica, with a dozen ornaments and a small, chipped manger scene underneath, stood in the far corner.

"Fuimos a la segunda." *We went to the second-hand store,* Rosa explained before he could ask how they could afford the tree. The local thrift stores often slashed their prices during the holiday season.

"I helped." Daniel shot Alberto a proud smile.

"Me too," Yesica squealed.

He clapped his son on the back and bent down to give Yesica a kiss.

It wasn't much, but it was theirs.

Bills spread out across their bed like an expensive quilt. Alfredo and Rosa poured over them, as if staring at them long enough would help them figure out an answer.

"*¿Y este? Ya lo pagaste, ¿verdad?*" *And this one? You paid it already, right?* Alfredo held up the cut-off notice from the electric company.

Rosa sucked in air through her teeth. "*Ay, ay, ay.*" She bumped the palm of her hand to her forehead in a pained look.

"*Ay, Rosa,*" Alfredo sighed. He looked at the due date. Yesterday. If they still lived in a large city like Guadalajara, the office would probably be open on holidays and the bus would be running to get them there. But they lived in a small city, tiny in comparison to the overcrowded metropolis where they grew up, so that meant they would need to wait until the day after Christmas. Their only hope was that the service person was off for the holiday, too. When it got cut off last time, they had a few days lag between the cut-off notice and the actual day he disconnected them from the transformer that powered the park.

They put the money for the bill in an envelope on their dresser and organized the rest of the bills into essential and non-essential piles. Yesterday, with Patty's help, they signed up for the sliding scale through the financial assistance program and then arranged to pay the hospital and its auxiliaries twenty-five dollars per month until the end of time, it seemed like.

The two piles were complete. Cable was always the first to go. They could let their minutes run out on their cells. They'd lose their numbers but phones weren't a necessity. Setting aside money for food, the water bill, and the bus, the rest would have to wait. They'd made it through harder times in Mexico, but there they had the emotional support of family. Here, they'd only been able to count on neighbors and coworkers as far as they could throw them.

The sooner he could find a job, the better. In the meantime, his family would have to survive by selling tamales at the local poultry plants and construction sites. They would be able to scrape by for a while, until people got tired of tamales or he found a job, whichever came first.

After transferring the piles of bills onto the dresser, Rosa got out a thin roll of wrapping paper, off-brand clear tape, the few quality presents she had picked up on sale throughout the year, and the cheap, dollar ones that would break after being played with a few times. Hiding the now-wrapped gifts in two grocery bags, they slid them back under the bed, leaving one present each for the children to open tonight.

Rosa checked on the tamales that were steaming on the stove, and Alberto loaded wet clothes into the dryer with his good arm. In the background, the television played a cartoon Christmas movie. The blender grinded in the kitchen as Rosa made her famous guacamole salsa, which sometimes earned as much as the tamales.

The trailer was alive with brightness and sound. Maybe it wouldn't be too bad of a Christmas after all. As soon as that thought crossed his mind, everything went black. The only thing that stayed lit was the battery-operated star on the top of the tree.

Daniel helped Alberto drag the heavy kerosene heater out of the hallway closet and set it in the center of the living room, turning the knob to the lowest setting. Rosa got the flashlights, and Yesica grabbed her princess blanket from her room. Snuggling on the couch with his family, Alberto pondered the sad fact that his children had zero reaction to the power getting shutting off and thought about how much worse things could get without him working. Disappointment in himself, and intense worry, crept into his heart, carrying a thick sadness.

In that moment, with the distractions of noise and lights no longer clouding their surroundings, the far-off clanging of a church bell entered the trailer. His mind traveled back to his childhood in Mexico, where the chiming was a daily ritual.

Dressed up in his Sunday best, his *Abuela's* warm, wrinkled hand in his, they stepped out from the cooler winter air into the sanctuary of Santa Cecilia. Surrounded by rich organ sounds and the overwhelming aroma of incense, the entire sanctuary was lined with hundreds of flickering candles that cast a soft, yellow light on the stained glass windows and dark wooden pews. Jesus, lit up on the cross behind the altar, stared at him as Alberto and his grandmother sang hymns celebrating His birth.

Outside their trailer, a car horn beeped, and Alberto shook the memory out of his head. Inside his heart, something longed to be unearthed. He looked at the time on his cell phone. Nine p.m. If they hurried, they could be dressed and walk to the church by the beginning of the Christmas Eve service. He took a deep breath and stood up.

Bundled up in scarves, hats, and mittens, they stepped through the door into the sanctuary, a familiar smell of *pozole* reaching their salivary glands. Smiling faces welcomed them like lifelong friends. They invited Daniel and Yesica to be part of the telling of the Nativity story. With Daniel strapping on sheep ears, a bushy tail, and a burlap sack with cotton balls sparsely glued on, and Yesica in a shimmery blue robe and halo, they joined the rest of the fidgety manger scene in the front of the church. Afterwards, they were invited to stay for *tamales* and *champurrado* and to play silly games into the wee hours of the morning.

In the end, that Navidad was not at all like any Alberto had experienced before. Sometimes God needed to use unusual methods to knock people out of their everyday routines and show them the Way. It took a group of carolers, a life-threatening accident, and their electricity getting cut off, but the Gonzalez family found a new home in that church and discovered something they never knew they were looking for: faith.

About the Author: Allison K. Garcia

Allison K. Garcia is the head of the Shenandoah Valley cluster meeting of the ACFW Virginia Chapter, is the Municipal Liaison for NaNoWrimo in the Shenandoah Valley, and a member of Shenandoah Valley Writers. Her short story, "At Heart," was published in the Winter 2013 edition of *From the Depths* literary magazine, along with her flash fiction. Her work, "You Shall Receive," was published in GrayHaven Comics's 2014 All Women's anthology. Allison won best story twice and several other prizes in Flash! Friday contests and an honorary mention in the ACFW Virginia 2015 Short Story Contest with "Just Another Navidad." Latina at heart, Allison has been featured in the local newspaper for her connections in the Latino community in Harrisonburg, Virginia. She also enjoys cooking real food for her husband and baby and spending time with the hermanos at her church.

Follow her at:

https://www.facebook.com/allisonkgarciaauthor

https://allisonkgarcia.wordpress.com/

@athewriter

allisonkgarcia@yahoo.com

The
Dance

by Kathleen Neely
(Honorable Mention)

You may not understand my lie. Especially if you are painfully shy, like me. The last thing in the world that I want to do is to draw attention to myself. I just want to blend in. Sure, I want to have friends and be accepted, but I don't want to stand out. My skirts aren't too short or too long, my jeans aren't skinny jeans, and I don't wear red. Rarely does my hand go up in school, even if I know the answers. It's the way I've always been, from as young as I can remember. When the spotlight is on me, my complexion turns bright crimson. I don't need a mirror to know. I can feel the red climbing to splotch my face. I hate when that happens, because it brings attention on top of attention. Double whammy.

So, take a girl who hates the limelight and move her at the beginning of her senior year to a school across the country. Does that sound like a cruel joke? Well, that's what my parents did to me. I know. Job. Transfer. No choice. Blah, blah, blah. I cried for three weeks. Couldn't Mom stay back with my sister Jodi and me, just for one school year? Couldn't I please just graduate from the school where I went all of my life?

Well, of course the answer was no. The move from Charlotte to Seattle might as well have been from Earth to Pluto. Oh wait, that's no longer the farthest planet because it's not really a planet anymore. How did they mess that one up for hundreds of years?

I wish I could be like Jodi. When she walks into a room, she owns it. She can talk to anyone, laugh, make jokes, ask questions. All the things that I can't do. If I try to intentionally say something funny, I feel sure that no one will know what I'm talking about, so of course they won't laugh. And worse than that is when I'm not trying to be funny, and everyone laughs. It is just safer to be me — uninteresting, invisible me.

But when you're seventeen and don't have a friend in the world, at least not here on Pluto, it stinks. So when Jamison and Maddie started to sit with me at lunch, I did my best to talk to them and somehow managed my complexion.

So, back to my lie. I said you wouldn't understand, but if you're in the small percentage of the population who are labeled "introverted," you just might. For about a week, I had a budding friendship with the two girls. We were sitting in the gym after school, watching the girls' volleyball practice. Well, as teenage girls tend to do, they began talking about all, and I do mean ALL, of the things that they are involved in. Jamison does drama and frequently gets parts in the community theatre, as well as landing the lead in the school's spring production. Maddie does gymnastics on a competitive level. Both play instruments, piano for Maddie and flute for Jamison. Add to that Key Club, Youth Group, and last year's mission trip to Costa Rica.

Sometimes you can stand out by talking, and sometimes you stand out for your silence. That was the case on the day of the lie. Still, I didn't have a lie planned ahead of time. I'm not aware of forming one in my brain or making my lips ready to speak it. The words just came out. When Maddie asked me if I played any sports or an instrument, I simply said, "I dance."

One lie is never enough. It always requires another. Both girls became super excited, peppering questions at me that I somehow answered with ease. What kind of dance do I do? Ballet and jazz mostly. Do I compete? Not since we moved. Did I find a dance troupe in Seattle? No, but I'm looking.

Then came the zinger. The words that brought the crimson climbing up to swallow my face. It came from Jamison.

"Oh Connie, I do ballet, too. You have to come talk with my director. We're performing *The Nutcracker* this Christmas. She's short of dancers and is scrambling to get all of the spots filled. Will you come with me next week to meet her? She'll be so happy to find another dancer."

Maddie looked at me with concern. "You okay, Connie? You look really red."

This was my out. "No, something that I ate didn't sit well. I think I better take off."

"You gonna be okay to walk home?" She touched my shoulder.

"Sure. The fresh air should help."

But I didn't make it out the door before Jamison called, "Tuesday. Mark that date and we'll pick you up. Your mom can come if she wants to talk with our director."

When I got home, I threw myself on my bed, lamenting how I had just messed up the only two friendships that I had in Seattle. I kept thinking of all of the reasons that I could give my mom for homeschooling me. Or maybe I could get some sickness, not really a serious one, of course, but something that would keep me home and have a homebound instructor. What I couldn't do was to go back to that school.

Jodi peeked into my room to tell me about her cheerleading tryouts, and to let me know that dinner was ready. I told Miss Popularity that I wasn't hungry. "Just tell Mom I'm not feeling well."

But, of course, that brought my mom hurrying to see what was wrong. I was pretty convincing that my stomach was sick. She even thought that my head felt warm. At least she didn't run for the thermometer. Well, I can assure you that my stomach would not be better tomorrow morning.

The Nutcracker. I saw it once, years ago. I barely remember all of the story, but I do remember how graceful and beautiful the dancers were. I was probably around ten or eleven. Going to my bookshelf, I ran my fingers over the spines.

With my door closed and my blinds drawn, I positioned my feet with legs crossed at the ankles, bent my knees, circled my arms aside my head, and performed a clumsy pirouette. Then another. And another. After about ten dizzying practices, I felt like I wasn't quite as clumsy. But that was a far cry from being a ballerina. I let the dizziness pass, then made a feeble, and I do mean feeble, attempt to stand on my toes and jump. Thankfully, I was close enough to the bed that it broke my fall, and I laid there laughing. It felt good to laugh after the awful feelings that had followed me since the lie. It also felt good to almost dance.

I flipped through the TV channels, looking for some old reruns of "So You Think You Can Dance." Finding one that aired at 8:00, I set my DVR to record it. It wasn't ballet but dance is dance.

Why I did the pointless practices or looked for the dance show is a mystery. I'm not a dancer, and I would die of fright being on a stage with people watching me. My dilemma had not changed.

My mom could always zero right in when something wasn't right. The next morning, when I told her that my stomach was still sick, she looked at me quizzically. "Are you sure there isn't something else going on, Connie?"

I assured her that it was just my stomach, and she let me stay home although I'm quite certain that I didn't convince her.

It was her book club morning, and I encouraged her to go. Once she was gone, I found *The Nutcracker* soundtrack on streaming music, turned it loud and danced. After spending half the night reading on the Internet about ballet positions and watching videos, I attempted to mimic some moves. It wasn't good, but it was fun. Just as a lark, I pulled my hair tightly and secured it in the back. It was only a tight ponytail, but from the front, I looked like a ballerina, minus the tights and tutu.

I about jumped off the planet when I heard my mother say, "So, I see that you're feeling better."

When in the world had she snuck in?

"Mom, you scared me half to death. I thought you were gone."

"Obviously." Her hands were positioned on her hips. She walked over and silenced the music spilling from my laptop, sat on my bed, and patted the spot beside her. I obediently joined her.

"What's going on, Connie? I know you aren't sick."

I dodged the question by asking one that I hadn't planned to ask. "Do you think that I'm too old to take dance lessons?"

Her eyes bored deep into mine. She let her question pass for now and talked about mine. "Well, you are never too old to learn something new, but why the sudden interest in dance? You never mentioned this before."

"I don't know. I just thought it would be kinda cool."

"Connie, you know that if you take dance, you'll have recitals. You'd have to dance for an audience. I know that's not your favorite place to be."

It wasn't, and the thought of it really did make my stomach sick. But something sparked inside of me when I did those first pitiful twirls. It just made me want to do more. And then they got better. Well, a little better.

"I know, but I kind of like dancing. And it's really good exercise," I added for persuasion.

"You don't have to convince me to let you take dance lessons. If you're interested, we'll give it a try. I just want you to know what you are getting into. And if you start it, you need to follow through."

I nodded. "Okay. I think I want to try it."

But my mom being my mom, she circled right back to the heart of the matter. "So, what's going on? Spill it, Connie."

Her words sounded authoritative, but I knew that she was soft for me. Usually more for me than for Jodi who would push her to the limits.

So I told her about my stupid lie. "It's just been hard here. And they both had so much that they do. My stupid, boring life was an embarrassment. I had to say something interesting. Besides, I don't really know where it came from. It just sort of blurted out."

"Sweetie, your life is not stupid and it's not boring. You just need to give this some time."

We were quiet for a minute, probably both thinking through what to do about the lie. I knew the right thing to do, but I just couldn't. It would be so humiliating to tell them the truth—that I lied because I don't have a life.

Mom spoke first. "Connie, no one can teach you to dance in a week. You can't try a few steps and be ready for *The Nutcracker*."

"I know that. That's not why I want to do the dance lessons. It's just that when I tried it, I knew it was something I want to do more. I know that I can't try out for the ballet. I just don't quite know how to get out of it."

"You could tell the truth. If those girls are your friends, they'll forgive you."

"Oh, right. Then they'll know how dorky I am, and I'll be back to no friends at all. I hate it here. I want to go back to Charlotte." I started to cry.

"You know that can't happen, sweetie. You've got to make the best of things. How about this. How about we go and meet the director. Tell her that you're interested in dance but have no experience. She can help us to find an instructor and give a little advice. Your friends will know that you talked with her, and you can simply tell them that it isn't the right time for you to make such a big commitment. No lies there. If you make a commitment to lessons, that won't leave enough time for a production."

"Thanks, Mom. Will you take me to meet her so I don't have to go with Jamison? That way, she won't know what we talked about."

So that was the plan. I told Jamison that my mom wanted to have a little more time talking so we made our own appointment. She was super happy, hugging me and saying what fun it was going to be to do *The Nutcracker* together.

Mrs. Baylor was amazing. She even made the phone call to set me up with an instructor at her practice and said that the one I would be with was just about the best instructor they had. We talked a little about *The Nutcracker Suite*, and I learned that, while the more accomplished dancers would get the leads, many novice dancers were featured in a few of the pieces. I assured her that I wasn't ready for even the lesser dance parts.

The next morning, I told a very disappointed Jamison that I felt rusty since I hadn't danced for a while, and that I would put my energy into lessons rather than performing. At least she didn't know that I lied.

I started my dance lessons with Greta, the instructor that Mrs. Baylor said was the best, probably because she was pretty strict. I had to do boring exercises and muscle strengthening over and over and unbelievably over. My hour and a half lesson consisted of one hour and fifteen minutes of tedious activities and fifteen minutes of a wonderful time to dance. I loved it more than all of the art classes or summer camps or activities that I ever did. The fifteen minutes when I was really dancing was worth all of the time that Greta pushed me. I could see a difference in the first two weeks. Greta never complimented me when she was driving me to challenge myself, but she always ended our lesson with a smile on her usually-firm face and a word of encouragement. After two weeks in her class, she said, "Connie, you're a natural. How is it that you never danced as a child? We have a lot of lost time to make up for, but you, my friend, are a dancer."

Mrs. Baylor stopped by during one of my sessions. She asked me to reconsider and take a part in *The Nutcracker*. I think my mom gave her a heads up on my shyness because she told me that I would be in the back row of dancers for just one very simple piece. It would get me a little stage experience. Even so, that terrified me. Plus, if I said yes, Jamison would see me dance and know that I'm a beginner. The word 'no' was on my tongue, but it just wouldn't come out. I wanted to say no, but I really wanted to dance. Well, dance won. So I would have one small part in *The Nutcracker*, and my lie would be found out. Jamison would see that I was a beginner and had never danced before.

The next week, we sat in the food court of the mall filled with Christmas shoppers. It was one week before Thanksgiving, but people seemed to have forgotten that holiday to start preparing for the big one. I was glad the girls asked me to shop with them, but a big black shadow followed me all day, just knowing that I had to tell them. I was to join the other dancers at rehearsal tomorrow. I couldn't delay any longer.

It was a little self-preservation to start by telling them about my painful shyness and how hard the move had been for me.

"My life just seemed so boring when I heard about yours. I was afraid if I was so uninteresting that you wouldn't want me hanging around."

Maddie said, "I can't believe that you thought you weren't interesting. When someone new comes, everyone is interested. It's like a mystery getting to know them. You didn't talk a lot like other girls, and that just added to the curiosity. I always thought you were interesting."

Jamison was kind of quiet, and I figured she was upset about my lie. And she should be. Friends shouldn't lie to each other, and they shouldn't try to make themselves look better than they are. I figured I had just lost a friend. Finally, she asked me a question.

"Connie, are you dancing now just to fit in? You don't have to do that. We're friends whether you dance or not. Friends whether you sing, or play tennis, or do cartwheels."

Relief warmed me like a mug of hot cocoa. "But that's just the thing. I know that the lie was wrong, but because of it, I started to dance. I love it so much that I can't stop dancing, whether I'm in the studio or in my bedroom. And I know it'll be a long time before I can be an accomplished dancer, but I'm having so much fun getting there."

Practice was after school, four days each week. I watched the girls who had been dancing all of their lives, many of them still in elementary school. They were so proficient that I wondered what in the world I was doing there. My mother watched me from the area where parents waited, and sometimes I would catch an encouraging smile. Still, I had this lump in my throat just thinking about opening night.

The director and stage helpers all talked about 'tech night.' Jamison said it was just a full rehearsal with lights and sound and staging. When I arrived, everyone was busy, moving things, calling out orders, and making last minute costume adjustments. Finally, we were ready. A handful of people sat in the audience. Blinding lights illuminated the stage, and there was some static from the sound system until they got it where they wanted it. This was a real production and, in two nights, all of the seats would be filled. That meant about 3,500 people from the floor to the third balcony.

The heat began rising to my head, and there was a heaviness in my chest. I felt like I couldn't get a breath and was afraid that my stomach might be sick. I wanted to run right down the aisle and out the door.

What excuses could I create? I could get sick, but Mom would see through that in a skinny minute. I could fall, not here where everyone would see, but home on the garage stairs or something. Maybe my ankle would swell up and even a doctor would say, "No dancing." I had to think of something, anything that would stop me.

I was so distracted that I didn't hear Jamison the first two times she called to me. "Sorry, what did you say?"

"I said, 'You'll do an awesome job, Connie.' You're so graceful you'll probably get a lead next year."

I smiled despite my nausea. It felt really good to hear that, even though I wasn't going to be dancing.

The next morning, I told my mom that I wasn't feeling well, and thought I should stay home from school. Her eyes narrowed and she looked at me with that scrutinizing glare; her no-nonsense mood.

Calmly, without raising her voice, she spoke. "No, Connie. Not this time. You're not backing out. You'll be at practice today and you'll be at Opening Night tomorrow."

"Mom, I didn't say I wasn't going there. I just said school. Maybe I should miss school today, you know, so I don't get worse."

A long stare, an uncomfortable length of silence, and she finally said, "Get dressed. The bus comes in twenty minutes."

And she just walked out my door.

Now what? Now I really was sick.

Later that day, the intercom buzzed into my classroom and called me to the office. They said I should pack for an early dismissal. I got a little worried because no one had said anything about picking me up today.

When I rounded the corner, my mom was in the office, signing me out.

"What's wrong?" But she didn't look like anything was wrong. She looked kinda' cheerful.

"Nothing at all. Just a little surprise."

We drove into town and parked in a garage not far from the Space Needle. Everything was decorated so beautifully for Christmas. Mom opened the car's trunk and pulled out two pairs of ice skates.

"Just a little mother—daughter time."

Cool. Did this mean that she wasn't going to make me go to practice? I had to ask.

"What about practice?"

"I'll have you there in plenty of time. Let's go have some fun."

Well, that had been wishful thinking, but at least I got out of school for a few hours and Jodi didn't.

I hadn't been skating in a while but was really pleased by how much better I had gotten. I guess dancing and skating have some things in common. We skated to *Jingle Bells* and *Jingle Bell Rock*. It sure put us in a holiday mood.

My mom kept up with me, but finally we both needed a break. We took off our skates and headed toward the large nativity that was set up. It was so lifelike, and we just stood there admiring it. The wise men had colorful clothes that looked rich with gold and gems. But it was Mary who stood out. Her beauty overshadowed all of the other figures. Mom must have had her eye on Mary, too.

"She's beautiful, but I'll bet the real Mary didn't wear a pretty, pink dress."

I agreed. "No, she wouldn't have looked like that after traveling all that way and not even having a room to stay in."

"She was a remarkable girl. Do you know that Mary was probably younger than you are now?"

"You're kidding, right?"

"No. Some scholars think she was about sixteen."

"Wow. I didn't know that. She must've been really scared."

"I'm sure she was. You know, they could have stoned her to death for being pregnant. Can you imagine going to your parents in that culture and telling them you were going to have a baby? And then going to your fiancé? That must have been terrifying."

"Yeah, but she didn't have any other choice. You couldn't..." I let the thought die on my lips because it was too unthinkable.

"Do you remember when Aunt Lucy was ready to give birth to Austin? How big she was?"

I laughed. "She was huge. All she wanted to do was sit with her feet up and every day she said, 'Please, God, let it be today.'"

"I doubt that Mary said that. She was probably praying the opposite. Please don't let it be here, on this dusty road. But I'm sure she was as uncomfortable as Aunt Lucy." We stood looking for a while and then my mom spoke very softly.

"My soul glorifies the Lord, and my spirit rejoices in God my Savior, for he has been mindful of the humble state of his servant. From now on all generations will call me blessed."

"That's what Mary said, isn't it?"

"Yes, Connie. Mary was 16 and frightened. But something miraculous happened to her, and it was greater than her fear. God had given her a gift, and rather than running from it, she rejoiced."

Now my mom was looking at me like she was talking to me, about me.

"Here's what I want you to remember. Anything worth doing is going to have some risk. It will make you uncomfortable. But you will be so sorry if you don't take that risk. And you will be so blessed if you do."

"I know you're right. I just get scared."

Mom reached out and took my hand, tracing my fingers with hers. She lifted my hand and placed it on my chest, right over my heart. "Feel the beat?"

"Yeah. I feel it, and when I get scared, I can feel it pounding." But I smiled while I said it.

"Honey, that pulse shows life. God wants you to live life to the fullest, and to rejoice in it. You have been given a miraculous gift. Dance is His gift to you. What you do with it is your gift to Him."

The stage represents the home of the Stahlbaum family on Christmas Eve. Beautiful ladies are dancing in a holiday spirit. Jamison in the forefront, and I, a novice dancer in the shadows, safely hidden in the back row with my hair pulled tightly into a ballerina's bun. I dance, not in celebration of Drosselmeyer's gift to Clara, not from the joy of the Nutcracker lying under the tree, but celebrating the freedom that comes as I gracefully move to Tchaikovsky's melody. It is greater than my fear. I am unmindful of the stage, the lights, and the audience. I am only aware of the dance.

About the Author: Kathleen Neely

 Kathleen Neely is a retired educator, wife, mother, and grandmother. After teaching elementary school, she moved into administration and worked as an elementary principal for Eden Christian Academy in Pittsburgh, PA, and for Shannon Forest Christian School in Greenville, SC. She is a member of ACFW and Cross N Pens, a local writing group. Her desire is to write wholesome fiction that honors Christ. A favorite scripture is Zephaniah 3:17--The Lord your God is in your midst, a mighty one who will save. He will rejoice over you with gladness, he will quiet you by his love, he will exalt over you with singing. (ESV) "How awesome is that!"

Twitter @NeelyKneely3628
kathyneely@gmail.com
Amazon.com/author/kathleenneely

Scripture quoted is New International Version, Luke 1:46-48

Christian fiction from HopeSprings Books

Women's Fiction:

"The Sheep Walker's Daughter" by Sydney Avey (and companion journal "The Wisdom of the Sheep Walker")

Pairs a colorful immigrant history of loss, survival, and tough choices with one woman's search for spiritual identity and personal fulfillment. Dee's journey will take her through the Northern and Central California valleys of the 1950s and reach across the world to the obscure Basque region of Spain. She will begin to discover who she is and why family history matters.

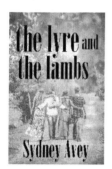

"The Lyre and the Lambs" by Sydney Avey

It's the Sixties. Modernity and tradition clash as two newlywed couples set up house together. Dee and her daughter Valerie move with their husbands into a modern glass house Valerie built in a proudly rural Los Altos, California, neighborhood. When their young relatives start showing up and moving in, the neighbors get suspicious. Then a body is found in the backyard and the life they are trying to build comes undone.

"Marriage Takes Three" by G.E. Hamlin

Darla Connor is struggling with whether to stay in her troubled marriage or walk away. Maintaining a long distance friendship with an old sweetheart isn't making the decision easier. Randall Connor is a recovering alcoholic and wants to heal his broken marriage. As a new believer, he is counting on God to help him.

When Darla rejects his ultimatum to sever ties with her old boyfriend, he's in for the battle of his life.

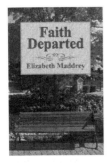

"Faith Departed" ('Remnants' series Book 1) by Elizabeth Maddrey

Starting a family was supposed to be easy.

Twin sisters June and July (pronounced "Julie") have never encountered an obstacle they couldn't overcome. Married just after graduating college, the girls and their husbands remained a close-knit group. Now settled and successful, the next logical step is children. But as the couples struggle to conceive, each must reconcile the goodness of God with their present suffering. Will their faith be strong enough to triumph in the midst of trial?

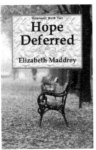

"Hope Deferred" ('Remnants' series Book 2) by Elizabeth Maddrey

Can pursuit of a blessing become a curse?

June and July (pronounced "Julie") and their husbands have spent the last year trying to start a family and now they're desperate for answers. As one couple works with specialists to see how medicine can help them conceive, the other must fight to save their marriage. Will their deferred hope leave them heart sick, or start them on the path to the fulfillment of their dreams?

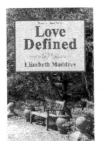

"Love Defined" ('Remnants' series Book 3) by Elizabeth Maddrey

Dreams Change. Plans Fail.

July (pronounced "Julie") and Gareth have reached the end of their infertility treatment options. With conflicting feelings on adoption, they struggle to discover common ground in their marriage. Meanwhile, July's twin sister, June, and her husband, Toby, are navigating the uncertainties of adoption and the challenges of new parenthood. How much stretching can their relationships endure before they snap?

"Mrs. Covington's Sunday School Dropouts" by Connie Miller Pease.

Cathy Covington has taught Sunday school to hundreds of young teens over the last forty years. After graduation, many of those students walked out the church door without a backward glance. Now Cathy is determined to see if a little nudge could push some of them back on the straight and narrow. But when Cathy is elected Chairman of the Lumberjack Days parade committee, her new post threatens to consume all her time and energy. And, as if life isn't crazy enough, she stumbles on a windfall that could change everything in her life. What follows is a hilarious, heartwarming adventure through the state forest, suburbs, and inner city as Cathy and her best friend Andi track down her former students, now troubled young adults. Along the way, Cathy learns that blessings have a way of hiding themselves until you are miles down the road, looking in the rear view mirror.

Contemporary Romance:

"Joint Venture" –Novella ('Grant Us Grace' series Book 0) by Elizabeth Maddrey

Laura Willis is busy planning her wedding to Ryan when she catches him cheating. Again. This time with her best friend. She throws her fist, and her ring, in his face and immerses herself in work at Brenda's House of Hair. But the salon is awash in drama too as Brenda cuts corners and goes on a rampage. Laura's coworker hairstylist, Matt Stephenson, is searching for other employment options and a new place to live. Deciding to take a risk, he determines to open his own salon and invites Laura to partner with him. Can their friendship survive the undertaking or will this joint venture be more than either of them bargained for?

"Wisdom to Know" ('Grant Us Grace' series Book 1) by Elizabeth Maddrey

Is there sin that love can't cover?
Lydia Brown has taken just about every wrong turn she could find. When an abortion leaves her overwhelmed by guilt, she turns to drugs to escape her pain. After a single car accident lands her in the hospital facing DUI charges, Lydia is forced to reevaluate her choices.

Kevin McGregor has been biding his time since high school when he heard God tell him that Lydia Brown was the woman he would marry. In the aftermath of Lydia's accident, Kevin must come to grips with the truth about her secret life. While Kevin works to convince himself and God that loving Lydia is a mistake, Lydia struggles to accept the feelings she has for Kevin, though she fears her sin may be too much for anyone to forgive.

"Courage to Change" ('Grant Us Grace' series Book 2) by Elizabeth Maddrey

Should you be willing to change for love?
When Phil Reid became a Christian and stopped drinking, his hard-partying wife, Brandi, divorced him. Reeling and betrayed, he becomes convinced Christians should never remarry, and resolves to guard his heart.

Allison Vasak has everything in her life under control, except for one thing. Her heart is irresistibly drawn to fellow attorney and coworker, Phil. Though she knows his history and believes that women should not initiate relationships, she longs to make her feelings known.

As Phil and Allison work closely together to help a pregnant teen, both must re-evaluate their convictions. But when Brandi discovers Phil's new relationship, she decides that though she doesn't want him, no one else can have him either. Can Phil and Allison's love weather the chaos Brandi brings into their lives?

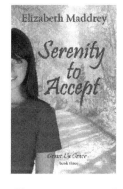

"Serenity to Accept" ('Grant Us Grace' series Book 3) by Elizabeth Maddrey

Is there an exception to every rule? Karin Reid has never had much use for God. There's been too much pain in her life for her to accept that God is anything other than, at best, disinterested or, at worst, sadistic. Until she meets Jason Garcia. After his own mistakes of the past, Jason is committed to dating only Christians. He decides to bend his rule for Karin, as long as she comes to church with him. As their friendship grows, both will have to decide if they'll accept the path God has for them, even if it means losing each other.

Historical Romance:

"Watercolor Dreams" by Sherry Kyle

He strolled into her painting . . . and into her heart.

It's 1910 and Anna Lewis is praying that God will help her become a premier watercolor artist of the lush beaches of Carmel, California. When a man strides down the beach and stops to face the ocean, Anna sketches him into her painting. Was it a mistake? Anna thinks so when he tells her he doesn't have spare change to purchase her work. Spare change indeed! But while she seeks God's leading for her art career, she'd better keep her day job as nursemaid to two rambunctious boys. The minute Charles Jordan walks away, he regrets criticizing the woman's painting but as he told the artist, he's just been jilted at the altar.How will a secret from Charles' past affect his chances of loving again? And how will Anna have the hope she needs when tragedy strikes and she must rely on the one man who crushed her spirit?

Romantic Suspense:

"Fiery Secrets" by Stephanie McCall

When it comes to trial, God either spares you from it totally, asks you to walk through it, or delivers you from it by taking you to Heaven. Dr. Grace Taylor, a driven pediatrician and single mom, needs divine intervention if she's going to heal from the actions of her cheating, abusive ex-husband. But she never thought God would work through Chris Anderson, a tutor at the local learning center whose secrets keep him from opening up to her. Both Grace and Chris have been asked to walk through their trial by fire; they've come out alive, but they still smell like smoke. Despite fears and distrust, love begins to take root in their hearts. But their fiery secrets threaten to keep them apart, and blister their souls.

Mystery:

"Not Guilty" ('Windspree' series, book 1) by Teresa Pollard and Candi Pullen

It's 1974 and Carrie Shepherd, daughter of the minister at Windspree Community Church, is a college senior with plans to be a missionary in Africa. Raped by a masked assailant, Carrie is so traumatized she tells no one until she realizes she's pregnant. Refusing to have an abortion, she must find the courage to face her family, her fiancé, her friends and a gossiping, angry congregation which may include her attacker.

"Not Ashamed" ('Windspree' series, book 2) by Teresa Pollard and Candi Pullen

Charity grew up as a missionary kid in Africa and is now a college freshman in America. Although she always knew there her dad was not her biological father, she was recently devastated by the truth that she was conceived in rape. Consumed with shame, she doesn't believe that her biological father has adequately paid for his crime and when she discovers a skeleton on the exact spot where her mother was attacked, she is convinced that her biological father is to blame. She launches an investigation with her uncle, the Chief of Detectives, who is equally convinced her father is not guilty. But can they catch the killer before he murders again?

Biblical Fiction:

"Tokens of Promise" by Teresa Pollard

Inspired by The Bible, Genesis 38, "Tokens of Promise" is an imagination of the love story of Judah and Tamar.

Rescued from disgrace by the handsome Judah, Tamar is already in love with the kind stranger. She eagerly followed Emi's advice on how to win him. It almost worked. He'd promised. If only his servant hadn't come at that moment, she'd be his wife now instead of going home with him to be his daughter-in-law. Why had her father agreed to this? Surely he could see her destiny was with Judah?

"Woman of Light: A novel inspired by the life of Deborah" by Teresa Pollard

Christian fiction inspired by the Bible, Judges chapters four and five. On his deathbed, Deborah's grandfather prophesied she would be a Judge for Israel. But the elders of Ramah vowed a woman would never sit in the city gates to listen to cases. So Deborah and her husband, Barak, returned to his hometown of Kedesh, in the northern part of the Israel, where trouble brewed nearby: King Jabin II had appointed Sisera to be commander of his army... and his nine-hundred iron chariots. Meanwhile, God brings disputes to Deborah for her to adjudicate, and soon she is holding court under the palm trees outside of Kedesh. Then God tells Deborah to hurry back to Ramah, and the family escapes just before Commander Sisera invades Israel and ransacks Kedesh. But Israel has no standing army to respond, and not a shield or a spear was seen among forty-thousand men. How will God use two such improbable people, a peasant woman and her husband, to lead Israel to victory against this formidable foe?

Speculative Fiction:

"A Message to Deliver" by Jeremiah Peters

Melissa is on a mission from God. With no memories of her life on Earth, she is immersed in a foreign world far different from her home in the paradise of Heaven. As Melissa struggles to discover the intended recipient of God's message, she simply tells everyone she meets the good news of God's love. Her new friend, Todd Simmons, blames abortion providers for the death of his mother. When an abortion clinic opens in the neighborhood, Todd starts down the path of vigilante revenge. As Melissa battles the influence of demonic forces, will she be able to save Todd and deliver God's message, or will the dark truth of her past lead her to abandon her mission?

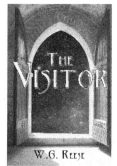

"The Visitor" by W. G. Reese

The divine blessings of Sior transformed the world of Ariel Leun into a paradise where people enjoy long lives in the company of mystical creatures. Winn, a transplant from the dark world of Draugh, reigns as a beloved King with his trusted advisor Caelan at his side, until the death of his Queen sends him spiraling into despair. Banishing Caelan and neglectful of his duties, King Winn is unaware that an old enemy, Garthpha, plots to take the throne. Rebelling against their father's retreat into seclusion, the heirs of Ariel Leun travel the passages of the Red Stone to Draugh where four warring Kings scheme to capture them, exploit their inner light, and deliver them to Garthpha as tribute. Can the children be rescued before their light is extinguished and evil takes the throne of Ariel Leun, plunging it into darkness?

Young Adult:

"Promise of a Future" by Stephanie McCall

College was supposed to be Kate McCune's first step towards independence. Instead, her cerebral palsy is in the spotlight now more than ever before. In fact, she's increasingly terrified her disability will soon make her life little more than a prison sentence. Kate's aunt, Elinor McCune, has distanced herself from an abusive childhood. Married to a wonderful man and pregnant, she is haunted by the specter of her past. When Kate's life derails, Elinor jumps in to help, and the two women begin a journey to make peace with the past and present. With dark forces threatening inside and out, they must find the road that leads to freedom and the promise of a future.

"Worth the Wait" (Waltham Academy Book 1) by Laura Jackson

Ellie Lansing has a picture-perfect life with a close-knit family and the perfect boyfriend. But her world is suddenly knocked off center when her drool-worthy boyfriend cheats, and her always-has-it-together mother is diagnosed with cancer. Ellie doesn't get it. She always does the right thing - doesn't God owe her a happy life? Through her heartache, Ellie learns that sometimes what seems like the end is really just the beginning and that what God has for us is always worth the wait.

"Worth the Time" (Waltham Academy Book 2) by Laura Jackson

Doesn't anyone feel she's worth their time? Routinely ignored by her single mother, high school senior Lindsey Hamilton hides her loneliness behind a mask of flirtatious self-confidence that has many boys wrapped around her finger. However, during community service required for graduation, she meets a shy guy with a haunted past who barely gives her the time of day. Why doesn't he like her? Then the father she thought had abandoned her before birth wants to meet, and she discovers everything she believed about him is a lie. How will Lindsey learn to trust so she can realize that she has been loved all along?

Tween fiction:

"Hear No Evil" ('Rustic Knoll Bible Camp' series Book 1) by Mary Hamilton

Summer camp is no fun for Brady McCaul. He fears that the girl with the cute dimples thinks he's immature and childish. The camp bully targets him with cruel taunts and teasing, and flips Brady's canoe to keep him from winning the race. But worst of all, his mom won't let him come home. She doesn't want him living with her anymore. Brady wonders if even God cares about him. Can Brady figure out what he did to earn Mom's rejection and change her mind by week's end? Or will he have to live with his workaholic dad, the guy who left when Brady was seven? All seems lost until a surprising secret changes everything.

"Speak No Evil" ('Rustic Knoll Bible Camp' series Book 2) by Mary Hamilton

Taylor Dixon knew having his younger sister at camp would be a pain, but he never expected the pain to go so deep. At 15, Taylor dreams of getting his driver's license and driving race cars when he's older. His sister, Marissa, is the only one who believes in his dream, but her adventurous spirit keeps landing him in trouble. Consequently, Dad won't let him get his license and predicts Taylor is heading for the same jail cell as his once-favored older brother. Taylor returns to Rustic Knoll Bible Camp expecting softball, swimming and sermons. Then he finds a classic Mustang in the camp's garage and jumps at the owner's invitation to help restore it. But when Marissa falls for his snobbish cabin mate, the war of words and pranks escalates until it threatens both the car and his dreams for the future. Will Taylor fulfill Dad's prediction and end up in jail? Or will he finally learn the Truth found in the old car's engine?

"See No Evil" ('Rustic Knoll Bible Camp' series Book 3) by Mary Hamilton

Steven Miller guards a dark secret. Dad drilled into Steven that blindness should never be used as an excuse. So when Steven finds an old triathlon medallion among Dad's belongings, he's inspired to follow in his footsteps. Maybe it'll quiet the guilt he's carried since Dad's death four years ago. While Steven continues his triathlon training during his final summer at camp, a serious illness keeps Rustic Knoll's beloved Nurse Willie from managing her clinic. When Steven teams up with his friend Claire to encourage Willie's recovery, his feelings for Claire grow beyond friendship. But his buddy, Dillon, has started down a dangerous path that Steven knows all too well. Can he keep his friend from falling into that sin without exposing his own past?

Short Stories

"Out of the Storm" Short Story Anthology

An anthology featuring the winners of the 2014 "Storming the Short Story" contest, sponsored by The Woodlands, Texas, chapter of The American Christian Fiction Writers (ACFW).

Contemporary category:

1st place: "Squall Line" by Jim Hamlett (Contemporary)
2nd place: "Dorothy's Carol" by Terrie Todd (Women's Fiction)
3rd place: "A Rumspringa Storm" by Steve Hooley (Amish)
4th place: "Tempest Tossed" by Annette O'Hare (Women's Fiction)

Speculative category (Fantasy / SciFi):

1st place: "The Grumpy Chronicles" by Susan Lyttek (Fantasy)
2nd place: "The Great Storm" by Karla Rose (SciFi)
3rd place: "Oddman" by Carla Hoch (SciFi)
4th place: "Aperture" by Linda Kozar (SciFi)

Other Genres category:

1st place: "Just West of Clovis" by Ralph D. James (Western)
2nd place: "Husband Hunting" by Crystal L. Barnes (Western)
3rd place: "Detention" by Gretchen Engel (YA / Fantasy)
4th place: "Fire in a Storm" by Angela K. Couch (Historical)

Proceeds from the sale of the anthology will be donated to the Scholarship Fund of the American Christian Fiction Writers (ACFW).

Connect with HopeSprings Books:
www.HopeSpringsBooks.com
Pinterest.com/chalfonthouse
Facebook.com/groups/ChalfontHousePublishingFans
Twitter: @HopeSpringsBook

49671815R00072

Made in the USA
Charleston, SC
01 December 2015